HORRORS IN HIDING

HORRORS
IN
HIDING

edited by
SAM MOSKOWITZ and ALDEN H. NORTON

A BERKLEY MEDALLION BOOK
PUBLISHED BY
BERKLEY PUBLISHING CORPORATION

First Mass Market Print... ... Black Cat... at 195...
... Pan, Reprinted by permission of the author...
...Doubleday, Garden City, N.Y., 19...

...August Dollar Magazine, 1933 by Ward
...from threatened agicultation of the author

CONTENTS

1. Introduction   11

2. Two Shall Be Born   15
   Seabury Quinn

3. Tell Your Fortune   45
   Robert Bloch

4. Time to Kill   76
   Henry Kuttner

5. Alannah   90
   August Derleth

6. Luana the Living   106
   Ray Bradbury

7. John Barrington Cowles   117
   A. Conan Doyle

8. The Door of Unrest   145
   O. Henry

9. Thrulow's Ghost Story   157
   John Kendrick Bangs

10. The Man With the Brown Beard   175
    Nathaniel T. Babcock

EDITORS' NOTE

This anthology is the fourth in a distinguished series by the editors, in which most stories have never previously been anthologized, and the combination of little known masterpieces by outstanding writers in the field of horror have earned both the acclaim of the critics and the support of the readers. Previous anthologies were *Horror Times Ten, Masters of Horror* and *Horrors and Hauntings.*

Sam Moskowitz is known as a researcher and scholar in the field of the fantastic and has authored many basic books on the history of science fiction, his latest *Under the Moons of Mars,* a hardcover history and anthology of science fiction in the Munsey magazines 1912 to 1920.

Alden H. Norton is a veteran editor of such nostalgic fantasy magazines as *Astonishing Stories, Super Science Stories, Famous Fantastic Mysteries* and *Fantastic Novels,* who has a weakness for this type of material.

INTRODUCTION

The title of this collection, *Horrors in Hiding*, is intended
to convey a double meaning. First, it is hoped to present
the readers with an outstanding set of thrills contrived
through the ingenuity of nine authors with diverse styles
and literary approaches. Secondly, and most important, it
is in the most deliberate possible sense, a selection of horror masterpieces little known and unknown, only one of
which has ever been reprinted before and even that one
never in an anthology.

The process of literary rediscovery is divided equally
between the old and the new. There are many reasons why
fine stories are "lost," and literary archeologists must set
forth periodically to do some real digging and unearth
them. Each story has a preface, giving its original place of
publication and something about the author. This
background material, with its sidelights on old periodicals,
special printings and author peculiarities, as well as its
relation of editorial idiosyncracies and biographical
highlights of the authors, should be read first. On the older
stories, in particular, it will suffuse the reader with the ex-
ultation of personal discovery and enhance the pleasure
which comes from having a double reason for reading.

Most of the authors in this collection are very famous,
which makes first presentation of an outstanding work by

them all the more unusual. But there is always a reason, and usually a very good one.

The late Seabury Quinn was so closely identified with Jules de Grandin, the occult detective, which he created, that the great body of excellent work he produced in the field of the supernatural outside his deservedly famous series has been overlooked. "Two Shall Be Born" is a sample of Quinn's mature skill as a teller of terrifying tales, and undoubtedly will bring about a demand for others.

Robert Bloch catapulted to fame so suddenly that the sifting process through the 25 years of science fiction, fantasy and horror tales that preceded "Psycho" is still in progress. The elements that brought about his success are constantly being found in stories like "Tell Your Fortune" which is a truly baroque combination of lightness of handling, strangeness of characterization and tampered-with scale which tells one's *real* fortune along with the weight.

Somewhere along the line, Henry Kuttner achieved so pervasive a reputation as an author of science fiction that it was forgotten that in his early years he was primarily a horror-story writer. From a rare issue of *Strange Stories,* a little-known tale of a "familiar" yet never-fought war, with overtones of psychological terror has been reclaimed for publication.

August Derleth has long been acknowledged as one of the true craftsmen in the art of the strange and terrifying. However, he wrote a group of 17 stories under the pen name of Stephen Grendon, which have a special subtle difference that distinguishes them from the body of his other works. One of the best of them, "Alannah," has been included here.

Ray Bradbury is purported to have ripped up literally millions of words of fiction before he began to click with the pulp magazines and moved on to his present renown. Of those millions of words, there were a few thousand he regarded as worth salvaging and among them was a story titled "Lunana the Living" which he gave to an amateur publication shortly before he sold his first story.

Preceding the writing of Sherlock Holmes, A. Conan Doyle penned and sold many stories, some of them fantasies. Genius does not bloom overnight, it is there waiting to be recognized. The same brilliance of plotting, the same planned indirection as is found in Sherlock Holmes appears in "John Barrington Cowles," but who would suspect a story with a title like *that* to be one of the most artful expositions of the manifest evil in a beautiful woman to appear in print!

Anthologists are prone to be ghoulish. They frequently crib from one another rather than actually doing the understandably tougher job of reexamining the main body of previously unselected works by even authors as undeniably great as O. Henry. For years it has been claimed that O. Henry wrote but a single tale of the strange and supernatural, "The Furnished Room," and that milestone has been reprinted endlessly. A search through the body of his work has turned up a superb short story of outstanding literary merit on the theme of The Wandering Jew under the title of "The Door of Unrest." There is no way to check every book ever published, but it would appear that this is the first time the story has ever been anthologized, let alone discussed.

John Kendrick Bangs wrote 19 volumes about ghosts, but they were also supposed to be books of *humor* and therefore not worthy of being culled for possible prospects for preservation. Careful reading uncovers a story titled "Thurlow's Ghost Story," about the assignment of an author to write a ghost story for the Christmas issue of a popular magazine. This story possesses many ironical aspects that transcend the slick exchanges of dialogue to make it a real discovery.

If Nathaniel T. Babcock was ever a famous author, he has long since been forgotten, except by bibliographers. Ah, there's the rub. In a bibliography of thousands of fantasy stories published by the Munsey magazines—*The Argosy, The Cavalier, The All-Story, The Scrap Book,* etc.—his title "The Man With the Brown Beard" was the earliest listed. The dyed-in-the-wool collectors who owned this bibliography numbered only in the hundreds, but as the years lengthened into decades and they found "The Man With the Brown Beard" almost impossible to obtain, their thirst to learn more about it increased with the intensity of that of a man hopelessly lost on a waterless desert for days. To satisfy that "thirst," the story is presented here, with an unexpected "plus." It turned out to be a powerful horror yarn, well worth reprinting and reading!

That is the sum of it. This volume is precisely what claims to be: *Horrors in Hiding*. Stories frighteningly good that have been lost, overlooked or unfairly ignored while scores of repetitious anthologies were appearing. I hope the readers will concur that the search of the editors for this type of material was worth the effort.

TWO SHALL BE BORN

By Seabury Quinn

Seabury Quinn is dead now, and the reputation he still possesses rests most heavily on his long series concerning Jules de Grandin, the occult detective. An excellent collection of the de Grandin stories under the title of *The Phantom Fighter* appeared from Arkham House in 1966, but some of Quinn's finest tales of supernatural fantasy were not part of that series at all.

Through the years, Quinn had acquired a superb knowledge of human nature, coupled with an instinctive feel for color in phrasing, that permitted him to work a rich mosaic of life into the tapestry of his stories. Seabury Quinn was a story teller with a stylistic ability that was above average. He probably wrote too much—over 500 stories—but to the pulps who published him, he gave in story value and writing technique far beyond what might be commonly expected.

Some clue to his true potential was contained in his Christmas masterpiece "Roads." Though it is an adult fantasy which first appeared in *Weird Tales* for January, 1938, it is one of the most rewarding concepts of the origin of Santa Claus ever written and the only other Quinn book to be published (Arkham House, 1948). His long novelette of the repeated incarnations of two lovers through the ages, *The Globe of Memories (Weird Tales,*

15

February, 1937), first awakened readers to his capabilities outside of the Jules de Grandin series. From that point on he wrote a substantial number of stories of literary merit, some of which have been anthologized and others of which are destined to be.

Few of the followers of Seabury Quinn are aware of other long-lived detective series of his. *Weird Tales* once had a companion magazine titled *Real Detective Tales & Mystery Stories,* edited by Edwin Baird. The mystery magazine was far more profitable than *Weird Tales,* so Clark Jacob Henneberger, original founder of both magazines, sold his interest to his partner, J. M. Lansinger, in the summer of 1924. Part of the arrangement was that Edwin Baird, who also edited *Weird Tales,* would leave Henneberger and continue exclusively with *Real Detective Tales & Mystery Stories.* He was replaced by first reader and assistant Farnsworth Wright, and a special arrangement was entered into with an Indianapolis printer to keep *Weird Tales* alive.

One byproduct of the sale was that many of the authors who wrote for *Weird Tales* also wrote for *Real Detective Tales & Mystery Stories.* Among them was Seabury Quinn, who had already begun a series of stories under the heading *Washington Night's Entertainment,* featuring Secret Service Agent Major Sturdevant, a bearded, middle-aged man, and his sidekick Loomis of the Washington, D. C. office of the *Clarion-Call.* The series ran for several dozen sequences and then was followed by another concerning Professor Forrester, more scientific and occasionally true horror and otherworldly.

There is a great deal of exploration that remains to be done into the works of Seabury Quinn, and the result should be some forgotten masterpieces for the reader's enjoyment and the collector's delight.

TWO SHALL BE BORN

By Seabury Quinn

Two shall be born the whole wide world apart
And speak in different tongues and have no thought
Each of the other's being and no heed . . .
That some day out of darkness they shall meet
And read life's meaning in each other's eyes.
— Susan Marr Spaulding, *Fate*.

Cold weather had set in, and the quiet street was like a scene from a Christmas card in the November dusk. The moon was very bright; its radiance was powdered silver on the frost-encrusted grass. Soft light filtered through drawn curtains on the neatly-kept front lawns. Somewhere down the block a window had been left open and through it, very clear in the cool tranquil air, a radio picked up a broadcast from Havana, mandolins and violins mourning softly over a tango. The placid beauty of the night was like the sting of salt in a raw wound to Fullerton. "A sorrow's crown of sorrows," he repeated bitterly, "is remembering happier things." Yet what was there to do but remember? Life was flowing backward for him, there was nothing in the future save, perhaps, such patience as a living dead man might command while he waited the actual sundering of flesh and spirit.

For Henry Herbert Fullerton—"H.H.F." beloved of the sports writers and one-time All American left tackle, later South American explorer and still late stock broker —was dead. Not dead the way you were when skilled morticians gave death the appearance of a natural sleep and clergymen droned prayers above you and women wept while soft music was played. Oh, no, not that—the lucky ones died that way! He was just civilly dead—*civiliter mortuus*—a legal corpse, deprived of all the rights of manhood till the state saw fit to restore them. An exconvict.

Like one who sees a motion picture reeled through its projector in reverse he viewed the incidents that marked

17

the past twelve years. His return from the exploring trip, the offer of the partnership in Smathers, Dirk & Houghton, his partners' endless importunities to bring his friends in on "good things"; his marriage to Millicent with the church banked suffocatingly high with flowers and gawking crowds held back by the police escort. Later, their duplex apartment and the cocktail parties that they threw; whispered market tips and eager friends with avid eyes who fairly forced their money on him. Then October, 1929, the crash, the realization that his trustful friends were ruined, the all-night drinking bout at Gilotti's speak-easy, and the return to his house just in time to meet Millicent and Bob Houghton at the door.

They had laughed at his befuddled questions, made a mock of his remonstrances. "Hold the bag, sucker," Bob had flung across his shoulder as he helped Millicent into the car.

Hold the bag, eh? They'd run out on him, leaving him to face the music, would they? He'd show 'em! When the police picked Bob Houghton up there were four bullet wounds in him, each of which would have been fatal. Not bad shooting for a drunken man. And Millicent was screaming at him, mouthing curses like a fish-wife.

His lawyers pleaded the unwritten law, his drunkenness, finally advised a plea of guilty in the second degree.

Ten years the judge had said. Ten years at hard labor. And the warden took him at his word. No office work, no soft duties for this killer who but for wealth and influence might be waiting for the final summons from the death house. The rock pile, the machine shop and the laundry, these were his portion while the sands of time piled slowly to a pyramid of ten long years. Then they set him free, a ticket to the city in the pocket of his prison-made ill-fitting suit, and the mark of the ex-convict on him. A slight, lean man of thirty-six who looked fifty, gaunt-featured, pewter haired, with the empty, lusterless eyes of a dead man walking.

Millicent had divorced him. Served the papers on him in the penitentiary. With a grim smile he recalled her accusations, "—assault with a deadly weapon—conviction of a crime involving moral turpitude—" He let the case go by default. Everything she said was true. Once he had tried to kill her; he loved her then, loved her so he'd rather see her dead than gone with Bob Houghton. No matter now. When one is quits with life what difference does it make whether he is married or divorced?

He'd seen her yesterday down on the Avenue, gray eyes aglint beneath the crisping curls of auburn hair, a smart small hat trimmed with cock feathers, a double cross fox scarf draped negligently across her shoulders. She'd passed him by as if he were a bit of wind-blown street-trash, and he had wondered idly that the sight of her stirred neither longing nor resentment in him, that he could look so calmly in that coldly lovely face and feel no quickening of the pulses as he passed within hand's reach of this woman who had vowed to cleave to him through sorrow and adversity while they both lived.

"But," he reflected bitterly, "she kept her bargain. One of us is dead; dead legally—*civiliter mortuus.*"

The moonlight glinted on a spot of brightness in the walk before his house, and Fullerton grinned as he marked it. His neighbor up the street, the small dark man who'd moved into the vacant house three doors away, had put that bright tile in his sidewalk the same day he took possession of the premises. Fullerton had noticed it as he went out upon his daily morning walk, a square of brightly finished porcelain, not white nor yet quite green, but a sort of combination of the two, noticeable in the dull-gray of the paving blocks as a cardinal in a flock of blackbirds. It had a figure on it, too, a man with a jackal's head, like the figures of Anubis he'd seen in the museums. Odd that he should have set a bright tile like that in the gray-stone walk. But then—

Last night was Halloween, the boys in South Brooklyn were like their kind the world over. Out ringing doorbells, stealing trash-cans, blowing beans at unprotected windows. Among their pranks had been the transplantation of the bright tile from his neighbor's walk to his. Tomorrow he must take it back. Only the diffidence that made him shrink from meeting people had kept him from restoring it that morning.

He put his hand up to the curtain cord, but delayed pulling it. Freedom to open or shut doors and windows was still a luxury to be savored. "Old Lovelace hadn't served a hitch in the big house when he wrote

> 'Stone walls do not a prison make,
> Nor iron bars a cage.' "

he said ironically, speaking naturally to himself, as lonely men have done since time's beginning. "If he had—what the deuce?" He ended on an interrogatively rising note as a light delivery van crawled down the street, the driver leaning far out of the cab to scan the sidewalks bordering the roadway.

Opposite his door the car came to a halt, and the driver jumped down, crossed the strip of parking and bent down to examine the bright tile. Satisfied with his inspection, apparently, he called to his helper, and walked back to the vehicle, where he began to unlatch the chains holding up its tail gate. In a moment they had drawn out a long packing case and were lugging it up his walk.

"You must have made a mistake," Fullerton insisted as they beat upon his front door with a thunderous knock. "I haven't ordered anything—who's this for?"

The driver and his helper had regained their seats in the car, and looked back at him surlily. "For a man," replied the driver. "See?"

"No, I don't. What's his name and address?"

"Dunno, Mister. Our orders wuz to put that box down at th' door o' th' house wid a fancy tile in its front walk. Didn't have no name or number; just a house in dis block wid a fancy tile. If you ain't th' party it's just too bad, for we ain't luggin' that crate back. See?"

With a wheeze and rattle the old car got underway, and Fullerton was left with the unwanted parcel on his doorstep.

"Now what?" he asked himself. The box was oblong, made of light wood strips reinforced with cross-tied ropes.

20

There was nothing on it to identify its consignee or consignor. In shape and size it was much like the rough box used to encase the casket at burial. Fullerton felt a slight chill of apprehension as he looked at it. What was he to do with it? The driver had said it was for the man with the bright tile in his sidewalk. That would be his new neighbor. Obviously the thing was too heavy for him to move it unassisted—"But I can't leave it out here all night," he told himself, "it may hold perishable goods." Tentatively he leaned down and took the nearer corners in his hands. Surprisingly, the case moved toward him easily, and he realized it had castors fitted to its lower surface. That simplified things.

Pulling, tugging, panting a little from the exertion, he drew the box across the doorsill and into the front hall. There, it would be safe till morning—

Shoving it with his foot to make a clearance way for the front door, he was astonished at the ease with which it rolled across the polished floor. Not only rolled, but cannoned into the newel post of the staircase. The crackling sound of breaking wood was followed by the tinkle of smashing earthenware, and he looked ruefully at the object exposed by the shattered crate.

Where the box had staved in he could glimpse a dull-white surface scarred by a wide crack. It was hard to make the object out. From its shape it might have been a bathtub, but who'd make a bathtub of fragile earthenware, or encase it in a box unable to withstand a slight jar such as that which smashed this case?

"H'm, maybe I can fix the thing," he muttered, putting back the broken boards. "Perhaps I'd better not try, but—" He couldn't understand it, but a curiosity greater than his powers of resistance seemed to prompt him. Plainly as if he'd heard the words pronounced he became aware that the box held something he must see—quickly.

He drew the boards away, looked down at the baked-clay case they had concealed. Six feet in length it was, and in general appearance it resembled one of those old covered soap-dishes without which no toilet set of the late nineties was complete. The top was slightly convex and seemed joined to the bottom by a tongue-and-groove joint into which some sort of plaster had been set. An inch or so below the junction of the top and body ran a border of the egg-and-dart design familiar to Greek pottery of the common sort. The whole appeared to have been baked in a brick-kiln, but not thoroughly, for in several places the rough finish had chipped off, leaving pits and indentations on the surface, as though the baking process had added more of brittleness than strength to the clay.

With his knife he dug away the soft cement that sealed the vessel. In a moment he had loosened it and lifted back the top. "Good Lord, what's this?"

The light from the hall chandelier shone past him into the clay casket, and as he looked into the cavernous container he felt the breath hit hard against his teeth while while a jerking, pounding feeling came into his chest beneath the curve of his left collar-bone. He was looking full into the still calm face of a dead woman.

Carefully, stepping softly with that reverence which is the instinctive due of death, he stood the casket cover in the angle of the wall and looked again into the terra-cotta coffin. If what he saw was death it was a startling counterfeit of life.

She lay as easily and naturally in her clay coffin as though she slept in her accustomed bed. Tall she was and slender, perfectly proportioned as a statue wrought by Phidias or Praxiteles, golden-haired and fair-skinned as a Nordic blonde. From tapering white throat to slender chalk-white ankles she was draped in a white robe, the simple Ionic *chiton* of white linen cut in that austerely modest style of ancient Greece in which the upper portion of the dress falls downward again from neck to waist to form a sort of cape, masking the outline of the bosom and leaving the entire arms and points of the shoulders bare. Save for the tiny studs of hand-wrought gold which held the gown together at the shoulders and the narrow double line of horizontal purple stripes at the bottom of the cape her dress was without ornament of any sort. There were no rings upon the long slim fingers of the narrow hands that lay demurely crossed upon her breast, her narrow, high-arched feet were bare. A corded fillet of white linen bound her bright hair in a Psyche knot.

For a moment—or an hour, he had no way of telling, for time seemed pausing, and breathing with it—he stood looking at the lovely body coffined in the baked-clay casket. Like every normal layman he had an inborn horror of death, and instinctively felt frightened in the presence of the dead, but, somehow, this did not seem death.

It was, rather, the image of slumber, of live unconscious, waiting to be waked.

Yet, despite appearances, he knew that she was dead, and had been for a thousand years and more. He had seen coffins like the one she lay in at the museums. Explorers' spades had dug them from the Christian cemetery at Alexandria, relics of the vanished Roman Empire of the East. He recognized her simple, graceful costume, too. The narrow stripes of Tyrian dye that edged her cape bore witness to her status as a freeborn Roman citizen, the corded girdle at her waist proclaimed her a virgin. She must have lived—and died—before the rise of Islam in the Seventh Century.

Yet though she must have passed from life to death twelve hundred and more years ago so perfect was the mimicry of life, so absolute the counterfeit of breathing sleep, that he was afraid to move lest he waken her.

Gradually his reason reasserted itself. The old Egyptians had been skilled embalmers; he'd heard it said they knew a process whereby all appearance of mortality could be removed; not the crude pickling of mummification, but a technique which approached that practiced by embalmers of our day. Yet look as he would he could find no sign of the embalmer's work, no wound, no slit in the smooth skin, no scar or bandage.

Reverently he bent above the dead form in the coffin. Beside the body, almost hidden by a fold of the white robe, he saw a roll of something which appeared like parchment, and bending closer he could make out letters on it. This might give a clue to her identity and explain her marvelous defiance of the natural law of dissolution.

The rolled screed crackled in his hands. It was not parchment, he discerned, but something thin and almost transparent, like row on row of library mending tissue joined skillfully together. He recognized it, he had seen its like in the museums—papyrus.

The writing on it was in square black letters strung together without break, as if the whole message were one long word. "What language?" he wondered, looking idly at the characters. Egyptian? Not likely, they used picture-writing. Greek? Perhaps, but the letters didn't look like Grecian characters. He ran his eye along the topmost line:

NOVERINTUNIVERSIPERBREVIA.

"Gibberish!" he told himself disgustedly, then checked in mid-breath. No! The characters were Roman capitals, like the numerals on his watch, and suddenly he recalled having heard that it was not until comparatively recent days that words were written separately for convenience in reading.

Here was a clue. He hadn't looked inside a Latin book in almost twenty years, but— Frowning with the effort, he bent his gaze upon the opening letters of the message:

NOV—that might be an abbreviation for *nova,* signifying new, but that would make the next word *erin.* There wasn't any such word he remembered. Still—

Suddenly, as a figure hidden in a picture-puzzle becomes clear when it has been stared at fixedly for a time, the first sixteen letters of the line seemed to separate. There they were, in two words:

NOVERINT — UNIVERSI — Know everyone, know all men—

And the next three characters spelled P-E-R—*per,* meaning by—

Then BREVIA—these writs, these writings—

He was making progress now. It would be a long task, but the thing could be deciphered and translated. Plainly it was in the nature of a legal document, perhaps a statement of the dead girl's name and parentage.

For the first time in more than ten years he smiled with

eyes as well as lips. "I'll know more about you in a little while, my dear," he told her in a whisper. Then, even lower: "Sleep on, and pleasant dreams."

It was almost morning when he leaned back from his desk, utterly worn out with unaccustomed work, but too astounded to be conscious of fatigue. Crumpled paper lay about him on the floor, the ashtray was piled high with cigarette stubs, but on the desk lay his translation completed:

Know all to whom these writings come that I, known to the Greeks as Philamon, but to my fellow-followers of the Old Gods' worship as Harmichis, being of the olden blood of mighty Egypt and a sworn priest of the Old Gods, have caused the virgin Helena to fall into a deep sleep by the arts of my learning, wherefrom she shall not waken till one takes her by the hand and calls her name and bids her rise.

Now to whosoever sees these writings, greetings and admonition: It is my purpose to assume a like sleep unto hers when I have finished preparations for her safekeeping, and for mine own. But haply it may fall out that we wake in divers places, and that another than myself shall summon her from sleep. Now, therefore, stranger, be ye warned. The virg.n Helena is mine, and not another's, and should thou come upon her sleeping in her coffin, thou art charged to leave her as thou findest her, for if she waken at thy bidding, and looketh on thee with favor, know that I, Harmichis, servant of the Most High Gods, and a mighty man in combat, will seek thee out and do thee mortal battle for her, and as for her, should she look on another with the eyes of love, then she shall truly die by my hand, and not awaken any more, either at the bidding of a mortal man or otherwise, for bodiless and without hope of resurrection shall she wander in Amenti forever. I have said.

The more he read the document the crazier it sounded, and, paradoxically, the crazier it sounded the more logical

25

it seemed. His recollection of the history of the Roman Empire of the East was sketchy, but he remembered having heard that the old faith was kept alive by Coptic descendants of the original Egyptians, and that even today there are men who claim to have been initiated into the mysteries of Osiris and the lesser gods of Egypt. It seemed quite possible that this man who called himself Harmichis might have been a member of the old priesthood. There was small doubt that the Egyptian priests understood hypnotism, just as the Hindus did. That would account for the assertion that Harmichis "caused the virgin Helena to fall into a deep sleep by the arts of his learning."

Evidently this had been some sort of ancient version of a lovers' suicide pact. Harmichis, unable to marry the Greek girl, had hypnotized her—put her in a state of suspended animation—coffined her and had her buried in the desert sands. He had then intended to hypnotize himself, or have another do it to him and be buried by her side. Then at some predetermined time he would awaken, issue from his grave and rouse the sleeping maiden. "And just in case somebody beat him to it, he gave 'em timely warning to lay off," Fullerton ended aloud.

He lighted a fresh cigarette and bowed his head in thought. How long had the hypnotic sleep lasted? How long does it take for a hypnotically induced trance to become true death? Obviously she had not wakened in her coffin. There was no sign of a struggle. Quite as obviou ly she had not died of slow starvation while in a cataleptic state. She was slender, but with the slenderness of youthful grace, not the emaciation of starvation.

He shook his head and rose. If only what old Harmichis had wished were possible—if only he could take her by the hand and call on her to waken—

Once more he stood above the terracotta coffin, looking in the dead girl's calm sweet face. Good Lord, but she was beautiful! Her smoothly-flowing contours melted into lines of perfect symmetry, dark lashes swept the pure curve of her cheeks, her lips, still faintly stained with color, rested softly on each other. Unbidden, a verse from *Romeo and Juliet* came to his mind:

Beauty's ensign yet
Is crimson in thy lips and in thy cheeks,
And death's pale flag is not advanced there.

Scarcely realizing what he did he bent down and laid his fingers on one of the slim pale hands resting on the dead girl's breast. He recoiled in surprise. The hand was warm as living flesh, firm and lovely to the touch.

"All right," he murmured argumentatively to himself. "I'm crazy. So what? I'm going to try it, anyway."

How did you say "arise" in Latin? He thought a moment, then, his hand upon the girl's, his lips almost against the little low-set ear that lay framed in a nest of glowing gold-bright curls: *"Serge, O Helena!"* He wasn't quite sure that was right. Perhaps he should have said, *"Serge tu,"* but ... *"O Helena, serge!"* he repeated, louder this time.

A chill, not quite of fear nor yet of pure excitement, but rather from a combination of them, rippled through him, for with the repetition of the command the fingers in his stirred, curled up to take a light hold on his hand, and the bosom of the dead girl heaved as if in respiration. The waxen-smooth blue-veined eyelids were lifted slowly from a pair of almost golden eyes, and a faint suggestion of color swept upward through her throat and cheeks like a blush. Her calm lips parted, trembled in a broken little sigh.

She met his startled gaze with a long look of gentle trust. "Is it truly thou, my lord?" she asked in a soft whisper.

He looked down at her raptly, like a worshipper before a shrine, or a child to whom a glimpse of fairyland has been vouchsafed. Involuntarily he leaned toward her. The attraction was instinctive, elemental, unreasoning as the drifting down of autumn leaves which take their flight without consideration or knowledge of the botanical process involved. For a long, heart-stilling moment they looked into each other's eyes, and as he looked at her he felt the shell of rage and hatred for the world and all mankind which he has kept about him for the last ten years

27

begin to soften like a frozen river in the first spring sunshine.

"Helena!" he breathed almost inaudibly.

Her steadfast eyes were wide, star-bright with tears that came unbidden to their black-lashed lids, and her lips were trembling like an eager child's. "Is it truly thou, my lord?" she asked again.

Hell-broth simmered to a boil in Alexandria. It was the summer of the year 635, and everywhere within the ancient city of the Ptolemies dissention reigned. Fanatic monks and deacons of the orthodox religion mobbed heretics of the old Coptic Church. Copts burned the orthodox churches, and murdered monks and priests at every opportunity. From the ghetto where almost a hundred thousand Jews were barred in by intolerance of Greek and Copt there issued almost nightly raiding parties to avenge the insults heaped upon the Sons of Israel by daylight. The Roman governor hanged and crucified adherents to all parties with a fine impartiality, and confiscated lands and goods with even greater readiness. From the East came ominous reports of Islam's onward march; some said that Amrou, general of the Caliph Omar's Syrian armies, had already laid siege to Pelusium, guardian fortress of the boundary.

In an upper chamber of her father's house in the Museum Street the damsel Helena was seated, reading from a vellum scroll the romance of Hero and Leander. Of late there had been little else that she could do. Most of the city's four hundred theatres were closed by order of the governor, for wherever crowds assembled rioting was sure to follow. The streets and squares re-echoed to the march of mailed *protectorii*—soldiers of the Roman garrison— the baths no longer afforded a comfortable haven for exchange of friendly gossip.

> " . . . yonder shines the blessed light,
> Love-kindled to dispel the night
> And lead me, Hero mine, to thee,"

she read, her lips half forming the words as her eyes traced down the lines of boldly-formed Greek letters. "Yes, Judith?" she looked up as a small Negro maid paused at the door with a deep bow.

"If it please your ladyship the Copt Philamon waits below, and beg an audience."

Helena's smooth brow wrinkled in a frown. "Bid him begone," she answered. "Tell him I am at the bath, or in the theatre—"

"I have, your ladyship, but still he lingers obstinately, saying he will wait until it pleases you to see him."

"Does he, in very truth? Why, then, 'twere better than I saw him quickly and dispatched the business for all time. Bring him hither, slave."

As the serving wench went on her errand Helena laid by her parchment and glanced toward the door with a small frown of annoyance between her classic level brows. Philamon—she had no wish to see him now or ever, yet for old time's sake she'd try to be as gentle as she might. They had been schoolmates and playfellows, though she was the daughter of a philosopher attached to the Museum and he the son of a rich Coptic merchant. Ostensibly he was a Christian, and bore the Greek name of Philamon, but as he grew from youth to manhood he had joined with others of his race in an attempt to revive worship of the ancient deities of Egypt. Until they had expelled him from the lecture halls of the Museum he had the impudence to preach the godhead of Osiris. Now, grown to man's estate, he presumed to sue for her hand—insolent desert-spawn, to aspire to the hand of one in whose veins ran the noblest blood of the Empire. The tinkling of the small bells on the silken curtain at the door cut short her reverie, and Philamon entered with a deep obeisance.

He was a handsome young man, dark, slender, lithe and almost silent as a snake in his movements. Above a tunic of deep Tyrian purple edged with gold embroidery he wore a light cape of green silk. A jeweled girdle with a dagger hanging from it in a sheath of gem-encrusted leather clasped his waist, buskins of white leather worked with

29

gold were on his feet. His curling black hair was encircled by a golden fillet.

"Salve, Helena," he greeted, dropping naturally into the classic Latin which, as a Copt, he preferred to the Greek spoken by the ruling class *"Dominus tecum."*

"Hast thou then become a Christian—again?" she asked with a faint sneer. "I had not thought to hear thee say—"

He cut her short with an impatient gesture. "There is no time to bandy words, my Helena. Knowest thou the latest tidings from the East?"

"What should a Grecian maiden know of them? Am I a Coptic traitor, having secret messages from spies—"

Once more his lifted hand broke through her bitter words. "Pelusium has been taken by Amrou. The path to Alexandria lies open to the hosts of Islam. Within the month the Caliph's soldiers will have ringed the city's walls with steel."

Now genuine alarm showed in her face. "The governor—"

"The governor? *Pah!*" He spat the exclamation out as though it were an epithet. "What can he do? The Roman soldiery is soft with too much wine and food, too little war. The Gothic mercenaries are besotted with their wine and dice and wenches, and would set sail for Europe ere the first assault. There is not a single legion in the field against the hordes of Amrou's Arab cavalry, and every day fresh troops of Saracens come up from Syria. There is no help or hope for it. The Alexandrian garrison is doomed."

"Then—then what shall I do?" she faltered.

He smiled. Not pleasantly. "Hear me, O Helena. Afortime I have offered you my hand, but you have refused—reviled—me. Now once more I make you offer of an honorable marriage and fortune which shall be secure from seizure by the Arabs. They have promised all us Copts immunity if we will join with them against the Greeks. I shall have high place and rank and power in the government of the Caliph. Which will you choose, O Helena, my name and love and fortune, or exile and poverty at the court of Heraclius? Philosophers are very plentiful in Byzantium. Thy father's learning will command small recompense."

Not for a moment did she doubt him. He was a traitor to the Empire, an apostate Christian, a conspirator, but no liar. In an agony of apprehension her fingers twisted and untwisted themselves. There was about her the appearance of a frightened child. "But I do not love thee, Philamon—"

"No more Philamon; I have done with all things Greek," he interrupted. "Call me by my rightful name, Harmichis."

She went on as if he had not spoken: "To wed a man not loving him—"

Once more he cut her short. "See, Helena, here is a window to the future. Look into it and tell me what thou see'st." From the pocket hanging at his girdle he produced a globe of rock-crystal somewhat larger than an orange and laid it on the table before her. "Look, look into it, my Helena, and see if thou wilt choose to be my mate, or brave the future unprotected!"

Timorously she bent forward, looking into the cool limpid depth of the glass ball. His eyes, hot; greedy, coal-black, were upon her, his sharp-cut lips were whispering insistently, "Look—look! Look through the window of the future, Helena—"

At first she saw no more than vague prysmatic mirrorings of the room, such as might have been reflected in a floating soap-bubble, but gradually the crystal clouded; shading from the clarity of water to the opalescence of fresh milk, then darkening steadily, appeared to grow jet-black, as if it were a sphere of polished ebony. A point of light appeared against the brilliant blackness, another, and another.

Now they were whirling round each other, like torches carried by wild-leaping dancers viewed from a tower top at night, and gradually they seemed to form a pattern. In their merging brightness she could decry figures—she saw the wild charge of the Arab cavalry, saw the Imperial legions staggering from the battlefield; beheld the great siege-engines set up under Alexandria's walls, and saw the Saracens come swarming up the battlements to cut down every living thing that barred their wild, victorious advance.

"Oh—horrible!" she faltered, and tried to wrench her gaze away from the bright sphere, but a power greater than her own will held her fascinated eyes upon it. A light, bright mist, an endless network of converging lines seemed taking form in the crystal. In its depths, as through a dim, wiped-over window, she beheld herself asleep. Asleep? No, never maiden slept in such a bed as that, save in the last long sleep that knows no waking. It was a coffin that she lay in, and they had taken all her jewelry off, slipped the bright emeralds from her ears, drawn the rings from her fingers, even taken off her gold-embroidered sandals. Dead. She, Helena, was dead, and about to be buried like a beggar maid.

But what was this? Above the coffin which enclosed her bent a face. She did not recognize it, for the features differed from the features of the men she knew. It was finely drawn with rather high cheekbones, the mouth was wide and generous, the eyes a pale and smoky gray. Hardened by suffering it was, and scarred by the deep acid-cuts of cynicism, but instinctively she felt drawn to it, for she knew that it belonged to one who had an infinite capacity for love and kindness—and infinite need of them.

"Art thou—art thou to be my lord?" she asked tremulously. "Art thou he into whose hands I shall lay my heart like a gift—"

Harsh and dry and rasping with cold fury Harmichis' voice drowned out her timid question:

"Sleep, Helena. Fall thou in a deep and dreamless sleep which men shall take for death, and wake no more until thy hand be taken and thy name called—"

Four oxen, white and without blemish, drew the funeral car that held Helena's coffin from the Church of Holy Wisdom to the great Necropolis where Christian dead were buried. Two dozen lovely maidens robed in white and veiled with purple walked barefoot in the dust beside

32

the flower-burdened hearse, with the Patriarch of Alexandria and his train of deacons and subdeacons following in their gilded curricles drawn by white mules. At the grave the girls wailed piercingly and tore their faces with their nails, then cut their long hair off and threw the braided tresses on the coffin. With incense, bell and intoned prayer the churchmen laid her in the grave and went their several ways.

The burying ground lay silent in the fading moonlight. A soft low haze that swept up from the harbor shrouded tree and monument and mausoleum in a silvery unreal half-light as Harmichis and the two stout knaves he had picked up on the waterfront crept silently as wind-blown clouds across the broad lawns of the great Necropolis. "Dig here," Harmichis ordered, and at his command the villains turned the loose turf back.

The ornate coffin, ornamented with a frieze depicting scenes from the life of Saint Helena, lay but a foot or two beneath the sod. In fifteen minutes it was hoisted from the grave, its sealings of lime-mortar broken, and the lovely corpse exposed.

Working quickly, Harmichis undid the emerald rings from Helena's small ears, drew the jeweled rings from her fingers, unclasped the brooch that held the Persian shawl about her shoulders, unlaced the gold-embroidered buskins on her feet. "Take them," he tossed the loot to his helpers. "Their price will buy a jar of wine in any shop along the quay." Then, as the scoundrels pocketed the finery, "Bring on the other coffin."

It was a plain, cheap case of half-baked earthenware they lugged from the cart hitched beside the road, the sort of casket used by those just rich enough to bury their dead chested, but too poor to afford any but the meanest funeral furnishings. Into it they put Helena, then dropped it in the place of her elaborate casket, and heaped the broken earth upon it.

"Break this up and throw the pieces in the harbor," Harmichis ordered as he gave the fine coffin a kick. "Here is the balance of thy hire." He tossed a purse to them and turned away. Chuckling, he murmured to himself, "No grave robber will seek for buried treasure in that pauper's coffin. Sleep on my Helena; sleep on in blessed poverty until—"

Half an hour later he was in his own bed chamber. His Grecian clothes were laid aside and in their place he wore a gown of plain white linen, such as that the priests vowed to Osiris wore in days before the coming of the Greeks and Romans. Before him on the table lay the crystal ball which he had used to hypnotize the girl.

"Gaze, gaze, Harmichis," he bade himself. "Gaze, servant of the Most High Gods, gaze in the magic crystal, yield up thy being and sink thou in a sleep so deep that men shall take it for death till—" His voice failed slowly, sinking from a murmur to a whisper, finally to silence. His head fell forward on his arms—

The news that Philamon the Copt had died of grief for Helena the Greek girl spread through the city. His funeral was a simple one, for neither Greek nor Coptic priest would say a prayer for one who had admitted publicly he was apostate, a follower of the old gods.

Nevertheless, because he had been rich, and because his will requested it, they dug his grave a little distance from the grave where Helena the Christian maiden had been laid.

"Art thou truly he whom I did see aforetime in the gazing-crystal of the renegade Philamon?" the girl asked Fullerton, her golden eyes fixed questioningly on him.

He was suddenly aware that she did not speak English—but that he understood her perfectly.

"Of—of course, it's I," he answered stammeringly, "but—" in his excitement he let go her hand, and instantly her look of rapt attention changed to one of mild bewilderment. She said something in reply. Her words were musically soft and liquid, but what she said he no more understood than if she'd spoken in Chinese.

"May I help you?" he put out his hand again, and she laid hers in it with the air of a princess bestowing a rare gift. Like a radio dialed suddenly from a foreign to a local broadcast, her words became intelligible in mid-syllable.

"—and Philamon—Harmichis—shall not have me?"

"He certainly shall not," he answered positively. "Neither he nor anyone, unless you wish—"

He stood away from her as he spoke, and once again he saw the puzzled look come in her eyes. She could not understand a syllable he pronounced.

Then understanding came to him. He could not explain it, but he knew. While they were standing hand in hand, or even when they touched each other lightly, everything one said was perfectly intelligible to the other. The moment they broke contact each was walled off from the other by the barrier of alien speech.

The maid had laid a fire before she left that evening, and in a moment he had kindled it. Then hand in hand they sat before the blazing logs and talked, and understood each other in that mystic communion which seemed to come to them when they made bodily contact. With only a few prompting questions she related her last day in Alexandria, told how Harmichis had bidden her look in the crystal— "The Saracens did not prevail against the soldiers of the Emperor, did they, my lord?" she broke off to ask him tremulously.

He took a deep breath. How could he tell her? But: "More than a thousand years ago, child," he answered.

"A thousand years—" Her eyes came up to his from under the deep shadow of their curling lashes. "Then I am—"

It was hard for him to explain, but adding what she'd told him to the information gleaned from the papyrus he could piece her history together. When he had done she bent her head in thought a moment. Finally she turned to him, eyes wide, lips parted. Her breath was coming faster. "I mind me that in that far day from which I come men sometimes found the mummies of the ancient ones in the rock tombs," she whispered.

"They're still doing it," he answered with a smile. "The mummies of Rameses and Tutankhamen are in museums—"

She nodded understandingly and he saw the pupils of her golden eyes swell and expand, darkening the bright irises. "To whom do they belong, those bodies salvaged from the past?" she interrupted.

"Why—to whoever finds them, I suppose," he rejoined, a little puzzled by her agitation.

"They are the things and chattels of their finders?" she persisted.

"Yes, I suppose you might say that—"

He stopped in utter surprise, for at his words the girl had slipped down from the couch and fallen to her knees before him. Taking his right hand in both of hers she bowed her head submissively and placed his hand upon it. "Full-ah-thon"—she said his name with difficulty —"behold me, a stranger from another age and place, alone and friendless in a foreign world. Freely, and of mine own will and accord, I give myself into thy ownership, and claim from thee the protection the master owes his slave. Take me, my lord and master; do with me as thou wilt. My life is in thy shadow."

He crushed down a desire to protest, or even show amusement at the drama of her self-surrender. She was a child of ancient days, and slavery was a social institution of her times. "Rise, Helena," he ordered solemnly. "I cannot take thee for my slave—"

Tears started to her lashes and rolled in big, slow drops down her pale cheeks, her lower lip began to tremble as though she were about to cry. "Am I then so favorless in thy sight that thou wilt not have me for thy handmaid, Full-ah-tohn, my lord?" she asked.

"Favorless? Why, child, you're beautiful; you're the loveliest thing I've ever seen—"

She was on the couch beside him now, her little feet tucked under her, one hand in his, the other resting on his arm. "Thou givest me my freedom, lord?" she asked.

"Of course, but—"

"But promise me one thing before I take it," she persisted.

"Why, certainly, if it will make you happier—"

"It will, my lord. 'Twill make me very, very happy. Each day at this same hour promise me thou wilt repeat those words—tell me that I am fair and lovely in thy sight!"

"You must be famished after your long sleep," he answered noncommittally. "Wait here, I'll boil some eggs and make some chocolate."

He was busy in the kitchen a few minutes, but busy as his hands were he was even busier with his thoughts. Here was a complication. This lovely girl who despite the date of her birth was physically no more than two and twenty had been literally dropped on his doorstep. In all the strange new modern world where fate had put her she knew no one but him; she was as utterly his responsibility as if she were a baby—and she had just demanded that he tell her she was beautiful at half-past three each morning.

A clinking sound as of metal striking stone attracted his attention as he bore the tray of food into the living room. Pausing at the front door, he looked out across the lawn.

Sharply defined in the moonlight, a man was working at the bright tile in his sidewalk, forcing it from its place with a light crowbar. As Fullerton's gaze fell on him the man paused in his labor and raised his head.

It was his new neighbor, the man before whose house the tile had been set. A shaft of moonlight striking through the unleafed boughs of a tree picked his face out of the shadow as a spotlight shows an actor's features on a darkened stage. It was a handsome face, with features clear-cut as an image on a coin, high cheekbones, a wide and full-lipped mouth and wide, black restless eyes with drooping lids and haughty, high-arched brows. Now it was convulsed in a frown of hot fury. He glared about him with a look of hatred sharp and pitiless as a bared knife, then once more bent to his labor.

Fullerton stepped quickly from the hall into the firelit sanctuary of the living room. There was a chilly feeling at his spine as he drew the curtains tighter over the windows.

He had, too, a curiously unpleasant feeling in the region of his stomach. Distinctly as if he were hearing them pronounced, he recalled the warning of the papyrus:

"—if she waketh at thy bidding and looketh on thee

37

with favor, know that I, Harmichis, servant of the Most High Gods of olden Egypt, will do thee battle for her." She had wakened at his bidding—did she look on him with favor? And if she did— He put the thought away deliberately, and placed the eggs and chocolate on the coffee table before her.

Fitting Helena into the modern scene was something of a problem at first. It was impossible to take her shopping in a costume which essentially was like a modern nightrobe, but Fullerton was equal to the emergency. He had her stand on sheets of paper and with a pencil traced the outlines of her feet. With these, and the help of an obliging saleswoman, he bought her a pair of shoes and stockings to accompany them. While she remained indoors enveloped in his bathrobe he took her *chiton* to a shop and bought a dress and cloak from its measurements. Thus clothed she sallied out with him, and for the first time in his life he understood why women love to shop.

The classic vogue in women's styles seemed to have been created for her benefit, she wore the latest modes as if they had been planned for her.

When the fashionable *coiffeur* put his shears to her knee-length hair she cried out as if he had cut her flesh with the keen steel, but when the process was completed and she emerged from the booth with her amber-blond hair waved up from neck and temples and a nest of curls massed high on her head she surveyed her image in the mirror with a gurgle of wide-eyed delight. "I did not think I was so beautiful," she confided to him. "Art sure"—she eyed him archly—"art sure thou wilt not reconsider and hold me to the offer which I made thee on the night thou wakened me?"

"What offer?" he asked, purposely obtuse.

She took his hand in hers and raised it. For the barest fraction of a second his palm brushed the bright curls that clustered like a crown upon her head. "If thou should wish to change thy mind—" she began. Then a salesgirl came with an armful of dresses, and the sudden tenseness which

38

had gripped his heart as if it were a giant hand relaxed.

It was almost incredible how quickly she learned English, and how readily she fitted into modern life. Eating with a knife and fork at first gave her a little trouble, she was superstitiously afraid of taxicabs and subways at first, and her first trip in an elevator terrified her almost to the point of swooning, but within a month she might have been mistaken for one of the season's crop of débutantes.

The change in him was almost noticeable as the transformation in her. The icy shell of rage and hatred which he had worn round him for the past ten years began to melt away as he found new interest in life. They went everywhere—did everything—together. To watch the changes in her face while they were at the opera or the play, to see the smiles break through the statuesque calm of her classic features when he introduced her to a new experience—the movies, a new food, horseback riding, skating on the frozen lake in Prospect Park, skiing in the Adirondacks—these things gave him pleasure of a sort he had not thought to know again. He and Millicent had never had much common interest. To Helena he was the sun around which all the worlds revolved. She looked to him for advice, guidance and protection. The feeling he was indispensable to someone gave him a new grip on life. He went to see his lawyers and had them prepare a petition to restore his civil rights. As soon as he was no longer a legal corpse he would initiate adoption proceedings. Helena—his daughter.

One of his first moves was to give up the house in South Brooklyn and take a new place on the Heights where they could look across the bay at the tall spires of Manhattan, bright with sunlight in the daytime, jewel-dotted with the glow of countless lighted windows after dark.

One April morning he drove through the block where he had lived when Helena was brought to him. His house was still vacant. FOR RENT signs hung in the windows. Three doors farther down the street he stopped his car and looked down at the sidewalk. The bright tile still twinkled amid the gray paving-blocks. "Too bad, old chap," he chuckled as he set the car in motion, "but there's no use keeping that thing there. Your date with Helena is off. But definitely."

A curtain stirred at a front window as he spoke, and for a second he glimpsed a face peering from the darkened house. It was the same face he had seen in the moonlight the night Helena came to him, but changed. Now it was like a skull that had been lightly fleshed over, a dead-white face with a blue growth of beard on cheek and chin, and narrow, venomous eyes.

Something—some unwonted sound must have awakened him, for he sat abruptly upright in the darkness, ears strained to catch a repetition of the noise. A sense of apprehension lay on him, in his inner ear a tocsin sounded an alarm insistently. Listening in the smothering darkness, he was not certain if he'd heard a sound, or if it were the sudden stopping of a sound that wakened him.

Then through the blackness of the darkened house it came again. A scream, a woman's scream so brief that he could hardly trust the evidence of his ears. A cry of stark and utter terror uncontrolled that stopped almost as quickly as it started, but seemed to leave a tingling echo of shrill horror quivering in the air.

Helena! The cry—if it had been a cry—came from the direction of the front room where she slept.

He fumbled in the darkness for a weapon of some sort. His hands closed on the first thing that they touched, a heavy flask of toilet water, and swinging the stout bottle like a club he ran on tiptoe down the hall.

A little trickle of dim light flowed out into the darkened hall beneath her door—as if someone had spilled a splash of luminance upon her floor and some of it had filtered across the sill.

Breathlessly, he bent his head to listen, laid cautious fingers on the doorknob. Voices, muted to a ghostly murmur, came to him from the room beyond.

"—but that was more than a full thousand years ago, Harmichis—"

A short, dry laugh, as frigid as a breath from an ice-cave, broke through the girl's low pleading. "Know'st not,

40

my Helena, there be three things which time is powerless to soften, a sword, a diamond and the hatred of a servant of the Olden Gods?"

"Nay, not hatred, surely, good Harmichis. Once thou dids't say thou loved me—"

Again the short, sharp, terrifying laugh. "As thou hast said, that was a thousand years ago, O Helena. Think'st thou I put thee in the mystic sleep to save thee harmless from the Saracen invader only to have thee fall into the hands of this outlander? Thou lovest him, dost thou not?"

"Yes, that I do; better than my life or sight or blood or breath, with all my heart and soul and spirit, but—"

"Then make thee ready for the sleep that truly knows no waking, Helena. This time thou'lt have no second chance. No other man shall take thy hand and call thy name and bid thee rise to live and love, for thou'lt be dust. Bare thy white throat to the knife of my vengeance—"

Fullerton drove in the door with a tremendous kick. On the floor beside her bed knelt Helena, her hands upraised to implore mercy from the man who towered over her, winding one hand in her glowing hair and holding a short copper-bladed knife against her throat with the other.

He recognized the intruder, the handsome, dark-skinned face, lean to emaciation, the lips drawn back in a reptilian smile of hatred about to be satiated—Philamon — Harmichis — the Egyptian priest whose love had driven him to hypnotize this girl so that she slept a thousand years, and who had followed her across those years to—

The Egyptian had hurled the girl down to the floor so violently that she lay in semi-consciousness, her hands stretched out before her like a diver's when he strikes the water, and turned on him. His teeth were very white against his swarthy skin, the hatred in his eyes was like a living thing. "Now, outlander!"

"You bet it's now!" Fullerton drew back the heavy bottle. "You're overdue in hell a thousand years—"

The bottle hurtled through the air with devastating force, missed the Egyptian as he dodged with weasel-like agility, smashed with a shattering crash against the wall, and—he was unarmed as the other advanced slowly, knife upraised.

Fullerton snatched up a slipper-chair and held it like a shield before him. Not a moment too soon, either, for the copper-bladed sacrificial knife, heavy with a grip of gold-encrusted lapis lazuli, came whining at him, struck the chair seat with a vicious *pung,* pierced it almost as if it had been cardboard, and thrust its needle point a full six inches through the fragile wood.

He hurled the chair at his advancing enemy, heard it crash with splintering legs against the wall as the other dropped to one knee, then felt his ankle seized as in a snare as the Egyptian slid across the floor and grasped him in a flying tackle.

They fell together in a thrashing heap, rolled over flailing, gouging, punching, digging at each other's eyes and clutching for each other's throats. Despite his slenderness the Egyptian was slightly heavier, and fought with the wild desperation of a mad man. But the years of heavy labor Fullerton had put in while he served his sentence stood him in good stead now. With a heave he drew the other to him, hugged him as a bear might hug its prey, and rolled until he felt the wiry body under him.

"Now, you damned desert rat—"

He felt a searing pain rake his right forearm, then his left, the coat of his pajamas ripped to tatters, and a line of bright blood marked the rents made in the fabric. From some hidden pocket in the linen smock he wore, Harmichis had jerked out a copper weapon like a set of brass knuckles, but armed with curving razor-bladed claws instead of knobs on its rings.

Now his face was roweled by the tear-talons—he could taste the salty blood upon his tongue, for the blades had cut clear through his cheek—in a moment they would reach his throat, his jugular.

With an effort calling up his final ounce of strength he rose to his knees, tottered to his feet, dragged the other after him, hurled him off with all his force.

"Get up!" His voice was hoarse and croaking in his own ears, choked with blood and all but stifled with the pounding of his heart. "Get up, you truant from hell's fire, and fight like a man!"

He stumbled toward the Egyptian who lay sprawled on his back, his head bent forward at a seemingly impossible angle, a look of utter, shocked surprise upon his face.

"Get up!" he repeated, seizing the supine man's throat. "Get on your feet and fight, or I'll—"

Then he saw it. From the corner of the Egyptian's mouth a little stream of blood welled, slackening and growing with each failing labored palpitation of his heart.

The fellow lay with his back pressed against the bottom of the broken chair, and the knife—his knife—that had pierced through the flimsy wood had struck deep in his back and pierced his lung when he fell on it.

Fullerton began to laugh. A ghastly laugh that rose and trilled and mounted like a shriek of sheer hysteria. "Caught in his own trap—taken in his own net—killed with his own knife!" he almost screamed, and staggered, sagging to his knees with loss of blood and utter exhaustion.

The sounds of the world were coming back again, but slowly, softly, as from a great distance. He could hear the casual noises of street traffic, the hooting of a taxi's horn, the rumble of a subway train as it slid into Clark Street station; far away the low, melodious belling of a Staten Island ferry's whistle.

Somebody bent above him. Somebody bathed his bleeding lacerated cheeks with sweet cool water, someone cried until her tears fell like a benediction on his upturned face. "O Full-ah-tohn, my lord, my life, my only love!" the syllables were thick with tears, but freighted with a very agony of adoration. "Arise, awake, my breath, my heart, my thrice-beloved—"

"You're asking me to wake—as I did you, my dear?" he answered weakly.

"Oh, yes, beloved, speak and tell me that you will not die—"

"Helena!"

She bent above him tenderly. Her hair was on his

43

forehead, her breath was cool and sweet against his cheek.

"Yes, Full-ah-tohn?"

"Will you—when I get well—will you marry me? I'm almost old enough to be your father, but—you've given me something to live for—you've—"

"Hai!" Her delighted exclamation interrupted his whisper avowal. "Thou old enough to be my sire, O Full-ah-tohn? Dost thou not realize I am a full thousand years thy elder?"

He was too weak to rise, but with her arm beneath his neck, her hands behind his head to guide it, and her lips to find his, he could kiss her.

And in that kiss there was the lighting of another hearth-fire, the hanging of another crane.

TELL YOUR FORTUNE

By Robert Bloch

It has been said that horror and humor are reverse sides of the same coin. Tragedy is all the more poignant if accompanied by an element of the grotesque. Robert Bloch's best work is an outstanding case in point. Humor in fiction or wit as a master-of-ceremonies has ever been his forté. During the depression, he worked in small Midwestern nightclubs as a stand-up comedian. His earliest success in writing came as a specialist of pure terror in the tradition of H. P. Lovecraft, but he soon was writing a parade of fantastic humor in *Fantastic Adventures* magazine, in a series revolving around Lefty Feep.

Sometimes during the Forties, these two elements began to coalesce and Bloch produced a series of horror stories whose impact was made all the more potent by an element of flippancy. The editor of *Weird Tales,* Dorothy McIlwraith, took note of this and when "Tell Your Fortune" was published, she made it the lead story of the May, 1950 issue.

The novelette follows a modern trend. It has elements of the mystery story, with possible explanations hovering between coincidence and the supernatural. Along the route popularized by the Dick Tracy detective strips, it features bizarre or off-beat individuals to add color to the story. Pete Mosko, as a 300-pound, ruthless, amoral gambling-den proprietor, makes an extremely effective villain, and Tarelli, the Italian mechanical wizard who may or may not have a direct-line to Hell itself, is a sympathetic noble figure in bondage.

Long after he made his reputation, Bloch like many other fine writers is now enjoying the luxury of having the genesis of that reputation discovered by anthologists and critics through stories such as this one.

TELL YOUR FORTUNE

By Robert Bloch

The scales aren't here any more. Look, Buster, I don't want any trouble. I run a nice quiet little place here, no rough stuff. I'm telling you—the scales aren't here. You must be the twentieth guy this week who come in looking for those scales. But they're gone. Damned good thing, too, if you ask me.

No, I'm not the bouncer. I'm the manager. So help me, I am. If you're looking for Big Pete Mosko, he's gone. Tarelli's gone too, and the girl.

Didn't you read about it in the papers? I thought everybody knew it by now, but like I said, guys keep coming in. The heat was on here for a month before I bought the place and made the fix. Now I run it strictly on the percentages; I level with the customers. Not like Mosko with his crooked wheels and the phoney cubes. Look the house over. No wires, no gimmicks. You want to make a fast buck at the table, you get your chance. But the sucker stuff is out. And I wouldn't be caught dead with those scales in here, after what has happened.

No, I don't think you're nosey. I'll take that drink, sure. Might as well tell you about it. Like I say, it was in the papers—but only part of it. Screwiest thing you ever heard of. Matter of fact, a guy needs a drink or two if he wants to finish the story.

If you come in here in the old days, then you probably

remember Big Pete Mosko all right. Six feet four, three hundred pounds, built like a brick backhouse, with that Polack haircut and the bashed-in nose. Don't like to give anyone the finger, but it looks like Pete Mosko had to be that big to hold all the meanness in him. Kind of a guy they'd have to bury with a corkscrew, too. But a very smart apple.

He come here about three years ago when this pitch was nothing but a combination tavern and bowling alley. A Mom and Pop setup, strictly for Saturday nights and a beer license. He made his deal with the county boys and tore out the bowling alley. Put in this layout downstairs here and hired a couple of sticks to run tables. Crap games only, at first. A fast operation.

But Mosko was a smart apple, like I say. The suckers come downstairs here and dropped their bundles one-two-three. Mosko, he stayed upstairs in the bar and made like your genial host. Used to sit there in a big chair with a ten-dollar smile plastered all over his ugly mush. Offering everybody drinks on the house when they come up from the cleaners. Let everybody kid him about how fat he was and how ugly he was and how dumb he was. Mosko dumb? Let me tell you, he knew what he was doing.

Way he worked it, he didn't even need to keep a bouncer on the job. Never any strong-arm stuff, even though business got good and some of the Country Club gang used to come out here and drop maybe a G or so at a time on Saturdays. Mosko saw to that. He was the buffer. A guy got a rimming on Mosko's tables, but he never got sore at Mosko. Mosko stayed upstairs and he kidded him along.

Show you how smart he was, Mosko played up his fatness. Played it up so he could be ribbed. Did it on purpose—wearing those big baggy suits to make him look even heavier—and putting that free lunch in front of himself when he sat in his chair at the end of the bar. Mosko wasn't really what you call a big eater, but he kept nibbling away at the food all evening, whenever somebody was around to look. Suffered something awful from indigestion, and he used to complain in private, but he put on a good show for the marks.

That's when he got a scale put in the tavern, to begin with. All a part of Mosko's smart act. He used to weigh himself in front of the suckers. Made little bets—fin or a sawbuck—on what he weighed. Lost them on purpose, too, just to make the marks feel good.

But that was an ordinary scale, understand. And Mosko was running an ordinary place, too—until Tarelli came.

Seems like Mosko wasn't content just to rim suckers on the dice tables. If his appetite for food wasn't so good, he made up for it in his appetite for a fast buck. Anyhow, when he had the bowling alleys ripped out downstairs, the carpenters built him a couple of little rooms, way in back. Rooms to live in.

Of course Mosko himself lived upstairs, over the tavern. These rooms weren't for him. They were for any of Mosko's private pals.

He had a lot of private pals. Old buddies from Division Street in Chi. Fraternity brothers from Joliet. Any lamster was a pal of Mosko's when the heat was on—if he had the moola to pay for hiding out in one of those private rooms downstairs. Mosko picked up a nice hunk of pocket money hiding hot items—and I guess he had visitors from all over the country staying a week or a month in his place. Never asked about it; you didn't ask Mosko about such things if you wanted to keep being a good insurance risk.

Anyhow, it was on account of those rooms that Tarelli come here. He was out of Havana—illegal, entry, of course—but he wasn't a Cuban. Eytie, maybe, from the looks of him. Little dark customer with gray hair and big brown eyes, always grinning and mumbling to himself. Funny to see a squirt like him standing next to a big tub of lard like Mosko.

I saw him the day he arrived. I was working for Big Pete Mosko then, bouncing and keeping the customers quiet. Mosko never talked about his little private deals handling

48

hot characters in the back room, and I clammed up whenever I was with him—it was strictly business between us. But even though I kept my mouth shut, I kept my eyes open, and I saw plenty.

Like I say, I saw Tarelli arrive. He got off the five-spot bus right in front of the tavern, just at twilight. I was out front switching on the neon when he ambled up, tapped me on the shoulder, and said, "Pardon. Can you inform me if this is the establishment of Signor Mosko?"

I give him a checkup, a fastie. Funny little guy, about the size of a watch-charm wearing a set of checkered threads. He carried a big black suitcase, holding it stiff-armed in a way that made it easy to tell he had a full load. He wasn't wearing a hat, and his gray hair was plastered down on his head with some kind of perfume or tonic on it which smelled like DDT and was probably just as deadly.

"Inside, Buster," I told him.

"Pardon?"

"Mosko's inside. Wait. I'll take you." I steered him towards the door.

"Thank you." He gave me the big grin—full 32-tooth salute—and lugged the keister inside after me, mumbling to himself.

What he could possibly want with Mosko I didn't know, but I wasn't being paid to figure it out. I just led him up to Big Pete behind the bar and pointed. Then I went outside again.

Of course, I couldn't help hearing some stuff through the screen door. Mosko had a voice that could kill horse-flies at five hundred feet. He talked and Tarelli mumbled. Something like this:

"Finally made it, huh? Rico fly you in?"

"Mumble-mumble-mumble."

"All set. Where's the cash?"

"Mumble-mumble."

"Okay. Stay as long as you want. Rico tells me you can do a few jobs for me, too."

"Mumble-mumble-mumble."

"Brought your own equipment, eh? That's fine. We'll

49

see how good you are, then. Come on, I'll show you where you'll bunk. But remember, Tarelli—you stay out of sight when customers are here. Don't want you to show your profile to any strangers. Just stick downstairs and do what you're told and we'll get along fine."

That told me all I needed to know, except what Tarelli was going to do for Big Pete Mosko while he hid out from the law in the basement back rooms. But I found out the rest soon enough.

Couple of days later, I'm downstairs stashing liquor in the storage room and I come back through the crap table layout. First thing I see is a couple of roulette wheels, some big new tables, and little Tarelli.

Tarelli is sitting on an orange crate, right in the middle of the wheels and furniture, and he's having himself a ball. Got a mess of tools laying around, and a heap more in his big black suitcase. He's wiring the undersides of the tables and using instruments on the wheels, squatting on this crate and grinning like a gnome in Santy Claus's workshop, I hear him mumbling to himself, and I figure it's only sociable I should stop by and maybe case the job a little.

He pays me no attention at all, just keeps right on with his wiring, soldering connections and putting some small batteries under the wheels. Even though he grins and mumbles, I can tell when I watch his hands that Tarelli knows what he is doing. The little foreign character is a first-class mechanic.

I watch him slip some weights under the rims of the three roulette wheels and it's easy to see that he's bored holes through them for an electric magnet below the Zero and Double-Zero, and then—wham!

Something smacks me in the back of the neck and I hear Big Pete Mosko yelling, "Whaddya think you're doing here? Get out before I break your lousy neck!"

I took the hint and ducked, but I learned something, again. Big Pete Mosko was putting in three crooked roulette wheels, and business was picking up.

Sure enough, less than a week later the tables were

installed and ready for action. I kept out of the basement as much as possible, because I could see Mosko didn't want anybody around or asking questions. I made it my business to steer shy of Tarelli, too. There was no sense asking for trouble.

Must have been all of ten days before I saw him again. This was just after the wheels were operating. Mosko brought in two more sharpies to run them, and he was taking them into town one afternoon, leaving me and the day bartender on duty. I went downstairs to clean up, and I swear I wasn't getting my nose dirty. It was Tarelli who started it.

He heard me walking around, and he come out from his room. "Pardon," he said, "Pardon, signor."

"Sure," I said. "What's the pitch?

"Ees no pitch. Ees only that I weesh to explain that I am sorry I make trouble between you and Signor Mosko."

"You mean when he caught me watching you? That's all right, Tarelli. He loses his temper—I'm used to it. Guess I shouldn't have butted into his business."

"Ees dirty business. Dirty."

I stared at him. He was grinning and nodding, but he wan't kidding.

"Feelthy!' He grinned harder. "I hate of myself that I do thees for Signor Mosko. For cheating people. Ees feelthy! That I, Antonio Tarelli, would come to such an end—"

"Take it easy, Buster. We all gotta live."

"You call thees living?" He shrugged at me, at the tables, at the cellar, at the whole damned world. "I come to thees country to make new life. Rico, he tells me I can do good here. Signor Mosko, I pay him the monies, he weel arrange. Ees no good. I am—how you say?—without help. I must do as Signor Mosko tells. He discover I am craftsman, he makes me do thees dirty work."

"Why don't you blow out of here, then? I mean, it's none of my business, but why don't you just scram right this afternoon? Even if Mosko plays it below the belt and hollers copper, you can get away into town and take a room. Nobody would find you. Lotsa guys in this country on illegal entry; they make out. Like I say, Tarelli, I'm not trying to advise you. But if you don't like crooked dealing, better leave and leave fast. How about it?"

Tarelli cocked his head up at me and grinned again. Then he squeezed my arm.

"You know sometheeng? I like you. You are honest man."

That was a laugh. But who was I to argue with a dumb foreigner? I just grinned back.

"Look," he mumbled. "Come, I show you why I not leave here right away now."

He took me down to his little room—an ordinary little room, with a rickety old bed, a straight chair, a second-hand dresser, and a dirty rug on the floor. "Come een," he said, and I stepped inside.

I wish somebody had cut my legs off, instead.

Tarelli went to the closet and dragged out his big black suitcase. He opened it up and pulled something out—a little picture, in a frame.

"Look," he said, and I looked.

I wish somebody had torn my eyes out, instead.

"Rosa," he mumbled. "Ees my daughter. Eighteen years. You like?"

I liked, and I said so.

I wish somebody had cut my tongue off, instead.

But I walked into his little room and looked at the girl with the black hair and the black eyes, and I told him she was beautiful and I sat there staring at her and he grinned and he spilled it all out to me. Everything.

I can remember almost every word, just as I can remember almost everything that happened from that afternoon on until the end.

Yeah, I learned a lot. Too much.

Let me boil it down, though. About Tarelli—he wasn't a lamster, in the old country. He was a Professor. Sounds screwy, but the way he pitched it, I knew he was levelling

52

with me. He was a Professor in some big college over there, university, I don't know what they call it. Had to blow during the war, got as far as Cuba, got mixed up in some mess down there, and then met Big Pete Mosko's pal, Rico. Rico got him into this country, which is what he wanted, and now he was looking for a way to latch onto a bundle.

"I am what you call financial embarrass," he said. "Rico, for breenging me here take all I have save up."

This I could understand. Any pal of Big Pete Mosko would be apt to be like that. A grabber.

"So now I work. Mosko employs the physicist, the most eminent of meta-physicians, to—rig, they say it?—games of chance. Ha! But I weel do anytheeng to earn money, to have Rosa here."

The deal was all set, I gathered. All Tarelli needed to do was scrape together a G-note and Rico would fetch Rosa on the plane. Easy as goniffing candy from a brat.

"So you're saving your pennies, huh?" I said, taking another look at Rosa's picture. "What's Mosko paying you for this machine job?"

"Twenty dollar."

Twenty dollars for a piece of work Mosko would have to pay easy two-three grand for if he got it done by any professional. Twenty dollars for three crooked wheels that would pay off maybe a grand or more a week clear profit. Big-hearted guy, Mister Mosko. And at that rate, Tarelli would have his Rosa over here just in time to collect on her old-age pension.

I took another look at Rosa's picture and decided it wasn't fair to make poor old Tarelli wait that long. Matter of fact, I didn't want to wait that long, either.

It wouldn't do much good to tell Tarelli that Mosko was playing him for a sucker. The thing to do was figure an angle, and fast.

I put Rosa's picture away. "We'll work something out," I said. "We got to."

"Thank you," said Tarelli.

Which was a funny thing for him to say, because I was talking to the picture.

I didn't have much time to talk to pictures the next couple weeks. Because Mosko had his roulette wheels operating, and the take was good. I kept busy quieting the squawkers, hustling out the phonies, and handling the guys who were sauced up. The two hotshots he hired to handle the wheels kept rolling.

Mosko was busy, too—just sitting in his office and counting the take. Must have been about two-three weeks after the wheels went in that I happened to pass his little private back office when Tarelli went in and gave him a pitch.

I couldn't help but hear what they were saying, because both of them were yelling pretty loud.

"But you promise," Tarelli was saying. "Rosa, she ees all alone. Ees not good for young girl to be alone. She must come here."

"That's your worry. Blow now, I got things to do."

"Theengs to do like counteeng monies? Monies you make from the crooked wheels I feex?"

"Never mind. Get outta here before I lose my temper."

"Ees worth plenty, thees job I do for you. Get Rosa for me. I pay you back. I work long, hard. Anytheeng you say."

"Blow."

"You must do sometheeng. You must!" Tarelli was almost bawling, now. "How you like, I tell somebody about crooked wheels?"

"Listen. One peep outta you and I tell somebody," said Big Pete Mosko. "I tell somebody about a guy who sneaked into this country without a passport. Get me?"

"You would not do thees!"

"Wait and see."

Everything was quiet for a minute. Way I figured it, things would stay quiet. Mosko had Tarelli, but good. If the little guy didn't watch his step, Mosko could turn him mover to the Feds. There was nothing anybody could do about it. Except—

"One theeng more—" Tarelli said.

"Blow."

"No. Leesten. Suppose I construct for you something very special?"

"How special?"

"Sometheeng—how can I tell you?—no one ever has before."

"Gambling device?"

"Perhaps."

"Cost money to make?"

"A few pennies."

"New, huh?"

"Special."

"All right, go ahead. We'll see."

"Then you weel send for Rosa?"

"We'll see."

Mosko let it go at that, and I didn't butt in. I was willing to see, too. And in another couple of weeks, I saw.

I was there the morning Tarelli took the wraps off his big secret. It was on a Sunday, and Mosko and the four sharpies who worked his wheels for him were downstairs, divvying up the take from the big Saturday night play.

Me and Al, the bartender, were sitting around in the tavern upstairs all alone, chopping the heads off a couple glasses of beer. There weren't any customers—never were on Sunday—so Al looked kind of surprised when he saw this little truck drive up and stop outside.

"We got company," he said.

"Company? Why, it's Tarelli," I told him.

Sure enough, little Tarelli hopped out of the truck and made some motions to the big lug who was driving it. The lug went around back and then he and Tarelli lifted down a big weighing machine. Before I knew what was happening, they dragged it into the tavern and set it up right in the corner.

"Hey," says Al. "Whatsa big idea?"

"Ees no idea. Ees scales. For weighing," Tarelli said, turning on his grin.

"Who ordered scales around here?"

Al come around the bar and we walked up to the weighing machine.

"I order," Tarelli told him. "I promise Mistair Mosko

to find sometheeng wonderful."

"Don't see anything wonderful about a penny scale machine," I said, giving it a fast case.

And there wasn't anything wonderful to see. It was just a regular weighing machine with a round clock-face glass front, and a pointer that spun up to 400 pounds, depending on who stood on it and dropped a penny in the slot. It was made by the Universal Scale Company of Waterville, Indiana, and the decal on the back said, "This machine property of Acme Coin Machine Distributors."

I noticed all this stuff kind of quick, without paying too much attention—but later, I memorized it. Checked up on it, too, when the time came, and it was all true. Just an ordinary weighing machine, made at the factory and rented out to Mosko for ten bucks a month plus 30 per cent of the take in pennies.

Oh, one other thing. Besides the big glass front over the dial showing the weight, there was another little hunk of glass and a spinner knob you turned when you dropped your penny. This knob turned about 20 slides up, for fortune-telling. You know, the regular questions you always find on scales. Like, "WILL I MARRY RICH?" Then when you dropped your penny, out comes a card with a gag answer on it, like "NO, YOU WON'T MARRY RICH. YOU'LL MARRY EDDIE." Corny stuff. And on top of the machine it said, "TELL YOUR FORTUNE—1¢ HONEST WEIGHT, NO SPRINGS."

Al and I looked at the scales and the guy driving the truck went away from there. Tarelli kept grinning up at us and at last he said, "How you like?"

"Phooey!" said Al. "Whatsa matter with you, Tarelli? You oughtta know better'n to louse up the joint with a penny machine. We got customers come in here to drop a big wad at the tables; you think they gonna fish out pennies to get their weight told?"

"Yeah," I said. "Does Mosko know you ordered this?"

"No," Tarelli answered. "But he find out fast."

"And he'll get sore faster," I told him.

"No he don't. You see."

"I'm gonna hate to see, Tarelli. When Big Pete sees this

56

phoney fortune-telling gimmick he'll go through the roof. He thought you were coming through with something big."

"Right. Thees ees of the most wonderful. Wait until I feex."

Tarelli waved at me and went downstairs. Al and I got back to our beers. Every once in a while Al would look over at the big, ugly white scales in the corner and shake his head. Neither of us said anything, though.

In a little while Tarelli come upstairs again. This time he was lugging his suitcase and a big canvas tarp. He set his suitcase down right next to the scales and then he got out a hammer and nailed up the tarp, right across the corner. It hid the scales and it hid Tarelli and his suitcase.

"Hey, now what you up to?" Al yelled.

"No questions. I feex. You cannot see."

"Lissen, you sawed-off little jerk—who you giving orders to around here?" Al hollered.

He got up, but I held his arm. "Take it easy," I said. "Give the little guy a chance. He's doing this for Mosko, remember? Maybe he's got some angle. Look what he did for the wheels."

"All right. But what's the big idea of the tarpaulin?"

"Secret," Tarelli called out. "Nobody must know. Three weeks I work to do. Ees miracle. You see."

We didn't see anything. We didn't even hear much of anything; some banging and clanking around, but not much. I guessed Tarelli was working on the weighing-machine with special tools from his suitcase, but I couldn't figure the angle. All I know is he worked on and on, and Al and I kept drinking beers and waiting for Big Pete Mosko to come upstairs and bust up the act.

But Mosko must have been plenty busy counting the take. He didn't show. And the fidgeting went on behind the curtain until Al and I were going screwy trying to figure things out.

"I got it!" Al says, at last. "Sure, I got it. Plain as daylight. Tarelli fixed the wheels downstairs for the big-time marks, diden' he? Well, this is for the little sucker—Mr. Bates, who comes in upstairs for a drink. We work the old routine on him, see? Plant a steerer at the

57

bar, get him into an argument about what he weighs, work him into a bet. Five, ten, twenty bucks. I hold the dough, get it? Then we take him over to the scales. Mr. Bates knows what he weighs, because before the showdown the steerer goes away to wash his hands, and I say to Mr. Bates, 'Quick, hop on the scales before he gets back. Then we'll know what you weigh for sure.' So the chump weighs himself and lets say he weighs 165. The steerer comes back and this time Mr. Bates offers to double or triple the bet. He can't lose, see? So the steerer falls for it and we have Mr. Bates for fifty or a hundred bucks. Then we weigh him official. And of course the scales says 170 or 175—whatever I want. Because I got my foot down on the pedal that fixes the scales. Get it? A natural!"

Somehow it didn't seem like such a natural to me. In the first place, no Mr. Bates was going to be dumb enough not to see through the routine with the crooked scales, and he'd raise a holy stink about being cleaned. Secondly, Tarelli had promised Mosko something really wonderful. And for some funny reason I had faith in Tarelli. I knew he was working to get Rosa over here—and he'd do anything for her. After seeing her picture, I could understand that. No, I expected Tarelli to come through. A big scientist, physicist or whatever kind of Professor he was in the old country, would do better than fix a weighing machine.

So I waited to see what would happen when Tarelli finished and took the tarp down.

Finally he did, and I saw—exactly nothing. Tarelli ripped down the canvas, carried his big back downstairs, and left the scales standing there, exactly like before. I know, because Al and I rushed up to look at the machine.

Only two things were changed, and you had to look pretty hard to realize that much. First of all, the little selector knob you could spin to choose your fortune-telling question just didn't spin any more. And second, the small glass-covered opening above it which gave the questions was now blank. Instead of printed questions like "WILL I MARRY RICH?" there was now a sort of

58

black dish behind the glass. It kind of moved when you got up close to it, as though it was a mirror, only black.

I know that sounds screwy and it was screwy; but that's the only way I can describe it. It was a little black disk that sort of caught your reflection when you stood on the scales, only of course you can't get a reflection off something dull and black.

But it was as if the scales were *looking at you.*

I hopped up and fished around for a penny. Closer I stood, the more I felt like something or somebody inside the scales was giving me a cold, fishy stare. Yes, and there was, come to think of it, a soft humming noise when I stood on the platform. Deep down humming from inside.

Al went around back and said, "Little jerk opened up the machinery here, all right. Soldered the back on tight again, though. Wonder what he was up to? Coin company's sure gonna squawk when they see this."

I found my penny and got ready to drop it in. I could see my reflection in the big glass dial where the weight pointer was. I had a kind of funny grin, but I guess that came from looking at the black disk below and listening to the humming and wondering about the wonderful thing Tarelli had done.

I held my penny over the slot, and—

Big Pete Mosko come running up the stairs. Tarelli was right behind him, and right behind Tarelli were the four sharpies.

"What's the pitch?" Mosko yelled. "Get off that machine and throw it out of here."

I got off the machine, fast. If I hadn't, Mosko would of knocked me off.

"Wait," Tarelli chattered. "Wait—you see—ees what I promise you. Wonderful."

"Scales!" Mosko grabbed Tarelli by the collar and shook him until his hair flopped all over his face. "What do I need with scales?"

"But they tell fortunes—"

"Tell fortunes?" Mosko began to shake Tarelli until it

59

looked like his hair would be torn right out of his head. "What do I need with phoney fortunes?"

"Ees—ees not phoney fortunes like you say. That ees the wonderful. The fortunes, they are true!"

"True?"

Mosko was still yelling, but the shaking stopped. He put Tarelli down and stared at him, hard.

Tarelli managed another one of his grins. "Yes, true. You get on machine. You put een penny. Fortune card comes out. Ees really true fortune. Tell your future."

"Malarkey!"

One of the sharpies, character named Don, started to laugh. He was a lanky blond guy with buck teeth, and he looked like a horse. In a minute we were all laughing. All but Tarelli.

"Take it easy, Tarelli," said Don, grinning and sticking out his big yellow teeth. He walked over to the little old man and stood looking down at him. It was funny to see the two of them together; Tarelli in his old overalls, and this sharpie Don in a handsome set of threads; new blue pinstripe job that matched the color of his convertible parked outside in the driveway. It was funny, and then it wasn't so funny, because the grin on Don's face was mean, and I knew he was just working up to something nasty.

"Look, Tarelli," Don said, still grinning. "Maybe you're a big scientist back in the University of Boloney or wherever you come from. But for my money, over here, you're just a schmoe, see? And I never heard that any scientist could invent a machine that really reads a person's future." Don reached down and patted Tarelli on the shoulder. "Now you know Mister Mosko here is a busy man," he said. "So if you got anything else to say, spit it out fast-like. Then I won't waste any more time before I kick you out in the road."

"Huh!" Mosko grunted. "I got no time for screwballs at all, Don. Telling what's gonna happen to you by science—"

"Ees not science." Tarelli talked real soft and looked at the floor.

"Not science?"

"No. I do anytheeng to get Rosa here, remember, I tell you that? I do what science cannot do. I make pact. Make vow. Make bargain."

"What kind of a bargain? With who?"

"I not say. My business, eh? But eet work. So I can build what I need for machine. Ees not science work here. Ees magic."

"What the—"

Mosko was yelling again, but Tarelli's soft voice cut him right off. "Magic," he repeated. "Black magic. I don' care who you are, what you are. You get on scales. Scales read your soul, your past, see you like you really are. Drop penny, scales tell your fortune. Read your future. Here, try eet—you see."

Then Don cut loose with his horse-laugh. Only this time he laughed alone. And when he shut up, Tarelli turned to Mosko again.

"Understan' what I tell you? Thees scale read the future. Tell anybody's fortune. Ees worth much money to have here. You can make beeg business from thees. Now you get Rosa for me?"

"Sure," said Mosko. "I'll get Rosa. If it works. Hey, Tarelli, whyn-cha get on the machine and see if it tells your fortune about Rosa? Maybe it'll say she's coming. Ha!"

Mosko was ribbing him, but Tarelli didn't know it. He turned kind of pale and stepped back.

"Oh no, Meestair Mosko. Not me! I not get on thees machine for anytheeng. Ees cursed, black magic. I do it only for Rosa— but I fear."

"Well, what we all wasting time standing around for?" Don snickered. "Tarelli's chicken. Afraid he'll get on the scales and nothing will happen, so we boot him out. Well, I'm not scared. Here, gimme that."

He snatched the penny out of my hand, hopped on the scales, and slid the penny down. I could hear the faint humming, and then when the penny disappeared I could hear the humming a little louder. The black disk on the scales got cloudy for a second. The pointer on the big dial behind the glass swung over to 182. Don stood on the

61

scales, 182 pounds of what the well-dressed man will wear, including his nasty grin.

"So?" he shrugged. "Nothing happens."

There was a click, and a little white card slid out of the slot below the black disk. Don picked it up and read it. He shook his head and passed the card to Mosko and the others. Eventually it got to me.

It was a plain white card with plain lettering on it—but it wasn't regular printing, more like a mimeograph in black ink that was still damp. I read it twice.

WHEN THE BLACK CAT CROSSES
YOUR PATH YOU DIE.

That's all it said. The old superstition. Kid stuff.

"Kid stuff!" Don sneered. "Tell you what. This faker musta gummed up the machinery in this scale and put in a lot of phoney new fortune-telling cards of his own. He's crazy."

Trelli shook his head. "Please," he said. "You no like me. Well, I no like you, much. But even so, I geev you the warning—watch out for black cats. Scales say black cat going to breeng you death. Watch out."

Don shrugged. "You handle this deal, Mosko," he said. "I got no more time to waste. Heavy date this afternoon."

Mosko nodded at him. "Just make sure you don't get loaded. I need you at the tables tonight."

"I'll be here," Don said, from the doorway. "Unless some mangy alley-cat sneaks up and conks me over the head with a club."

For a little while nobody said anything. Tarelli tried to smile at me, but it didn't go over. He tugged at Mosko's sleeve but Mosko ignored him. He stared at Don. We all stared at Don.

We watched him climb into his convertible and back out of the driveway. We watched him give it the gun and he hit the road. We watched him race by towards town. We watched the black cat come out of nowhere and scoot across the highway, watched Don yank the wheel to swerve out of its path, watched the car zoom off to one side towards the ditch, watched it crash into the culvert, then turn a somersault and go rolling over and over and over into the gully.

There was running and yelling and swearing and tugging and hauling, and finally we found all that was left of 182 pounds and a brand new suit under the weight of that wrecked convertible. We never saw Don's grin again, and we never saw the cat again, either.

But Tarelli pointed at the fortune-telling card and smiled. And that afternoon, Big Pete Mosko phoned Rico to bring Rosa to America.

She arrived on Saturday night. Rico brought her from the plane; big Rico with his waxed mustache and plastered-down hair, with his phoney diamond ring and his phoney polo coat that told everybody what he was, just as if he had a post office reader pinned to his back.

But I didn't pay any attention to Rico. I was looking at Rosa. There was nothing phoney about her black hair, her white skin, her red mouth. There was nothing phoney about the way she threw herself into Tarelli's arms, kissing the little man and crying for joy.

It was quite a reunion downstairs in the back room, and even though she paid no attention when she was introduced to me, I felt pretty good about it all. It did something to me just to watch her smiling and laughing, a few minutes later, while she talked to her old man. Al, the bartender, and the sharpies stood around and grinned at each other, too, and I guess they felt the same way I did.

But Big Pete Mosko felt different. He looked at Rosa, too, and he did his share of grinning. But he wasn't grinning at her—he was grinning at something inside himself. Something came alive in Mosko, and I could see it—something that waited to grab and paw and rip and tear at Rosa.

"It's gonna be nice having you here," he told her. "We gotta get acquainted."

"I must thank you for making this possible," she said, in her soft little voice—the kid spoke good English, grammar and everything, and you could tell she had class. "My

63

father and I are very, very grateful. I don't know how we are going to repay you."

"We'll talk about that later," said Big Pete Mosko, licking his lips and letting his hands curl and uncurl into fists. "But right now you gotta excuse me. Looks like a heavy night for business."

Tarelli and Rosa disappeared into his room, to have supper off a tray Al brought down. Mosko went out to the big downstairs pitch to case the tables for the night's play. Rico hung around for a while, kidding with the wheel operators. I caught him mumbling in the corner and dragged him upstairs for a drink.

That's where Mosko found us a couple minutes later. Rico gave him the office.

"How's about the dough?" he said.

"Sure, sure. Justa minute." Mosko hauled out a roll and peeled off a slice for Rico. I saw it—five Cs. And it gave me a bad time to watch Rico take the money because I knew Mosko wouldn't hand out five hundred bucks without getting plenty in return.

And I knew what he wanted in return. Rosa.

"Hey, what's the big idea of this?" Rico asked, pointing over at the scales in the corner.

I didn't say anything, and I wondered if Mosko would spill. All week long the weighing machine had stood there with a sign on it, "OUT OF ORDER." Mosko had it lettered the day after Don got killed, and he made sure nobody got their fortune told. Nobody talked about the scales, and I kept wondering if Mosko was going to yank the machine out of the place or use it, or what he had in the back of his head.

But Mosko must have figured Rico was one of the family, seeing as how he flew in illegal immigrants and all, because he told Rico the whole story. There wasn't many around the bar yet that early—our Saturday night players generally got in about ten or so—and Mosko yapped without worrying about listeners.

"So help me, it's truth," he told Rico. "Machine'll tell just what's gonna happen to your future. For a stinkin' penny."

Rico laughed.

"Don't give me that con," he said. "Business with Don and the cat was just a whatchacallit—coincidence."

"Yeah? Well, you couldn't get me on those scales for a million bucks, brother," Mosko told him.

"Maybe so. But I'm not scared of any machine in the world," Rico snorted. "Here, watch me."

And he walked over to the scales and dropped a penny. The pointer went up. 177. The black disk gleamed. I heard the humming and the click, and out came the white card. Rico looked at it and grinned. I didn't crack a smile. I was thinking of Don.

But Rico chuckled and handed the card around for all of us to see. It said:

YOU WILL WIN WITH RED.

"Good enough," he said, waving the card under Mosko's nose. "Now if I was a sucker, I'd go downstairs and bet this five hundred smackers on one of your crooked wheels, red to win. If I was a superstitious jerk, that is."

Mosko shrugged. "Suit yourself," he said. "Look, customers. I gotta get busy." He walked away.

I got busy myself, then. The marks started to arrive and it looked like a big Saturday night. I didn't get downstairs until after midnight and that was the first time I noticed that Rico must have kidded himself into believing the card after all.

Because he was playing the wheel. And playing it big. A new guy, name of Spencer, had come in to replace Don and he was handling the house end on this particular setup. A big crowd was standing around the rig, watching Rico place his bets. Rico had a stack of chips a foot high and he was playing them fast.

And winning.

I must have watched him for about fifteen minutes, and during that time he raked in over three Gs, cold. Played odds, played numbers. Played red, and played black too. Won almost every spin.

Mosko was watching, too. I saw him signal Spencer the

time Rico put down a full G in blue chips on black to win. I saw Spencer wink at Mosko. But I saw the wheel stop on black.

Mosko was ready to bust, but what could he do? A crowd of marks was watching, it had to look legit. Three more spins and Rico had about six or seven Gs in chips in front of him. Then Mosko stepped in and took the table away from Spencer.

"See you in my office," he mumbled, and Spencer nodded. He stared at Rico but Rico only smiled and said, "Excuse me, I'm cashing in." Mosko looked at me and said, "Tail him." Then he shook his head. "Don't get it," he said. He was working the wire now, finding everything in order.

Out of the corner of my eye I saw Rico over at the cashier's window, counting currency and stuffing it into his pocket. Spencer had disappeared. Rico began walking upstairs, his legs scissoring fast. I followed, hefting the brass knuckles in my pocket.

Rico went outside. I went outside. He heard my feet behind him on the gravel and turned around.

"Hey," I said. "What's your hurry?"

Rico just laughed. Then he winked. That wink was the last thing I saw before everything exploded.

I went down on the gravel, and I didn't get up for about a minute. Then I was just in time to see the car pull away with Rico waving at me, still laughing. The guy who had sapped me was now at the wheel of the car. I recognized Spencer.

"It's a frame, is it?" Big Pete Mosko had come up from downstairs and was standing behind me, spitting out pieces of his cigar. "If I'da know what those dirty rats would pull on me—he was working with Spencer to trim me—"

"You did know," I reminded him.

"Did I?"

"Sure. Remember what the fortune-telling card said? Told Rico, 'YOU WILL WIN WITH RED', didn't it?"

"But Rico was winning with both colors," Mosko yelled. "It was that dog Spencer who let him win."

"That's what the card said," I told him. "What you and I forget is that 'Red' is Spencer's nickname."

We went back inside because there was nothing else to do—no way of catching Rico or Spencer without rough stuff and Mosko couldn't afford that. Mosko went back to the tables and took the suckers for a couple hours straight, but it didn't make him any happier.

He was still in a lousy temper the next morning when he cut up the week's take. It was probably the worst time in the world to talk to him about anything—and that's, of course, where Tarelli made his mistake.

I was sitting downstairs when Tarelli came in with Rosa and said, "Please, Meestair Mosko."

"Whatcha want?" Mosko would have yelled it if Rosa hadn't been there, looking cool and sweet in a black dress that curved in and out and in again.

"I want to know if Rosa and I, we can go now?"

"Go?"

"Yes. Away from here. Into town, to stay. For Rosa to get job, go to school nights maybe."

"You ain't goin' no place, Tarelli."

"But you have what you weesh, no? I feex machines. I make for you the marvelous scale of fortune, breeng you luck—"

"Luck?" Rosa or no Rosa, Mosko began to yell. He stood up and shoved his purple face right against Tarelli's button nose. "Luck, huh? You and your lousy machine—in one week it kills my best wheel man, and lets another one frame me with Rico for over seven grand! That's the kind of luck you bring me with your magic! You're gonna stick here, Tarelli, like I say, unless you want Uncle Sam on your tail, but fast!"

"Please, Meestair Mosko—you let Rosa go alone, huh?"

"Not on your life!" He grinned, then. "I wouldn't let a nice girl like Rosa go up into town without nobody to protect her. Don't you worry about Rosa, Tarelli. I got plans for her. Lotsa plans."

Mosko turned back to the table and his money. "Now, blow and lemme alone," he said.

They left. I went along, too, because I didn't like to

67

leave Rosa out of my sight now.

"What is this all about, Father?" Rosa asked the question softly as we all three of us sat in Tarelli's little room.

Tarelli looked at me and shrugged.

"Tell her," I said. "You must."

So Tarelli explained about being here illegally and about the phoney roulette wheels.

"But the machine—the scales of fortune, what do you mean by this?"

Again Tarelli looked at me. I didn't say anything. He sighed and stared down at the floor. But at last, he told her.

A lot of it I didn't understand. About photo-electric cells and mirrors and a tripping lever he was supposed to have invented. About books with funny names and drawing circles in rooster blood and something called evocations or invocations or whatever they call it. And about a bargain with Sathanas, whoever that is. That must have been the magic part.

I guessed it was, because of the way Rosa acted when she heard it. She turned pale and began to stare and breathe funny, and she stood up and shook Tarelli's shoulders.

"No—you did not do this thing! You couldn't! It is evil, and you know the price—"

"Nigromancy, that ees all I can turn to to get you here," Tarelli said. "I do anytheeng for you, Rosa. No cost too much."

"It is evil," Rosa said. "It must not be permitted. I will destroy it."

"But Mosko, he owns the machine now. You cannot—"

"He said himself it brought bad luck. And he will never know. I will replace it with another scale, an ordinary one from the same place you got this. But your secret, the fortune-telling mechanism, must go."

"Rosa," I said, "you can't. He's a dangerous customer. Look, why don't you and your old man scram out of here today? I'll handle Mosko, somehow. He'll be sore, sure. but I'll cool him off. You can hide out in town, and I'll join you later. Please, Rosa, listen to me. Look, kid, I'll level with you. I'm crazy about you. I'll do anything for you, that's why I want you to go. Leave Mosko to me."

She smiled, then, and stared up into my eyes. She stood very close and I could smell her hair. Almost she touched me. And then she shook her head. "You are a good man," she said. "It is a brave thing you propose. But I cannot go. Not yet. Not while that machine of evil still exists. It will bring harm into the world, for my father did a wicked thing when he trafficked with darkness to bring it into being. He did it for me, so I must destroy it."

"But how? When?"

"Tonight," Rosa said. "Tomorrow we will order a new scale brought in. But we must remove the old one tonight."

"Tarelli," I said. "Could you put the regular parts back in this machine if you take out the new stuff?"

"Yes."

"Then that's what we'll do. Too dangerous to try a switch. Just stick the old fortune-telling gimmick back in and maybe we can get by for a while without Mosko noticing. He won't be letting anybody near it now for a while, after what happened."

"Good," said Tarelli. "We find a time."

"Tonight," Rosa repeated. "There must be no more cursed fortunes told."

But she was wrong.

She was wrong about a lot of things. Like Mosko not having any use for the fortune-telling scales, for instance. He lied when he told Tarelli the machine was useless.

I found that out later the same afternoon, when Mosko cornered me upstairs in the bar. He'd been drinking a little and trying to get over his grouch about the stolen money.

"I'll get it back," he said. "Got a gold mine here. Bigges' gold mine inna country. Only nobody knows it yet but you and me." He laughed, and the bottles rattled behind the bar. "If that dumb guy only could figure it, he'd go crazy."

"Something worked up for the fortune-telling?" I needled.

"Sure. Look, now. I get rich customers in here, plenty of 'em. Lay lotsa dough onna line downstairs. Gamblers, plungers, superstitious. You see 'em come in. Rattling lucky charms and rabbits-foots and four leaf clovers. Playin' numbers like 7 and 13 on hunches. What you think? Wouldn't they pay plenty for a chance to know what's gonna happen to them tomorrow or next year? Why it's a natural, that's what—I can charge plenty to give 'em a fortune from the scales. Tell you what, I'm gonna have a whole new setup just for this deal. Tomorrow we build a new special room, way in back. I got a pitch figured out, how to work it. We'll set the scales up tomorrow, lock the door of the new room, and then we really operate."

I listened and nodded, thinking about how there wasn't going to be any tomorrow. Just tonight.

I did my part. I kept pouring the drinks into Mosko, and after supper he had me drive him into town. There wasn't any play on the wheels on Monday, and Mosko usually hit town on his night off to relax. His idea of relaxation was a little poker game with the boys from the City Hall—and tonight I was hot to join him.

We played until almost one, and I kept him interested as long as I could, knowing that Rosa and Tarelli would be working on the machine back at the tavern. But it couldn't last forever, and then we were driving back and Big Pete Mosko was mumbling next to me in the dark.

"Only the beginning, boy," he said. "Gonna make a million off that scales. Talk about fortunes—I got one when I got hold of Tarelli! A million smackers and the girl. Hey, watch it!"

I almost drove the car off the road when he mentioned the girl. I wish I had, now.

"Tarelli's a brainy apple," Mosko mumbled. "Dumb, but brainy—you know what I mean. I betcha he's got some other cute tricks up his sleeve, too. Whatcha think? You believe that stuff about magic, or is it just a machine?"

"I don't know," I told him. "I don't know nothing about science, or magic, either. All I know is, it works. And it gives me the creeps just to think about it—the scales sort

70

of look at you, size you up, and then give you a payoff. And it always comes true." I began to pitch, then. "Mosko, that thing's dangerous. It can make you a lot of trouble. You saw what it did to Don, and what happened to you when Rico had his fortune told. Why don't you get rid of it before something else happens? Why don't you let Tarelli and Rosa go and forget about it?"

"You going soft inna head?" Mosko grabbed my shoulder and I almost went off the road again. "Leave go of a million bucks and a machine that tells the truth about the future? Not me, buddy! And I want Tarelli, too. But most of all I want Rosa. And I'm gonna get her. Soon. Maybe—tonight."

What I wanted to do to Big Pete Mosko would have pinned a murder rap on me for sure. I had to have time to think, to figure out some other angle. So I kept driving, kept driving until we pulled up outside the dark entrance to the tavern.

Everything was quiet, and I couldn't see any light, so I figured whatever Rosa and Tarelli had done was finished. We got out and Mosko unlocked the front door. We walked in.

Then everything happened at once.

I heard the clicking nose from the corner. Mosko heard it, too. He yelled and grabbed at something in the dark. I heard a crash, heard Tarelli curse in Italian. Mosko stepped back.

"No you don't!" he hollered. He had a gun, the gun had a bullet, the bullet had a target.

That's all.

Mosko shot, there was a scream and a thud, and then I got the lights on and I could see.

I could see Tarelli standing there next to the scales. I could see the tools scattered around and I could see the queer-looking hunk of flashing mirrors that must have been Tarelli's secret machinery. I could see the old back of the scales, already screwed into place again.

But I didn't look at these things, and neither did Mosko and neither did Tarelli.

We looked at Rosa, lying on the floor.

Rosa looked back, but she didn't see us, because she had a bullet between her eyes.

"Dead!" Tarelli screamed. "You murder her!"

Mosko blinked, but he didn't move. "How was I to know?" he said. "Thought somebody was busting into the place. What's the big idea, anyhow?"

"Ees no idea. You murder her."

Mosko had his angle figured, now. He sneered down at Tarelli. "You're a fine one to talk, you lousy little crook! I caught you in the act, didn't I—tryin' to steal the works, that's what you was doing. Now get busy and put that machinery back into the scales before I blow your brains out."

Tarelli looked at Mosko, then at Rosa. All at once he shrugged and picked the little box of mirrors and flashing disks from the floor. It was small, but from the way he hefted it I could tell it was heavy. When he held it, it hummed and the mirrors began to slide every which way, and it hurt my eyes to look at it.

Tarelli lifted the box full of science, the box full of magic, whatever it was; the box of secrets, the box of the future. Then he smiled at Mosko and opened his arms.

The box smashed to the floor.

There was a crash, and smoke and a bright light. Then the noise and smoke and light went away, and there was nothing but old Tarelli standing in a little pile of twisted wires and broken glass and tubes.

Mosko raised his gun. Tarelli stared straight into the muzzle and grinned.

"You murder me too now, eh? Go 'head, Meestair Mosko. Rosa dead, the fortune-telling machine dead, too, and I do not weesh to stay alive either. Part of me dies with Rosa, and the rest—the rest was machine."

"Machine?" I whispered under my breath, but he heard me.

"Yes. Part of me went to make machine. What you call the soul."

Mosko tightened his finger on the trigger. "Never mind that, you crummy little rat! You can't scare me with none of that phoney talk about magic."

72

"I don't scare you. You are too stupid to un'rstand. But before I die I tell you one theeng more. I tell your fortune. And your fortune is—death. You die too, Meestair Mosko. You die, too!"

Like a flash Tarelli stooped and grabbed the wrench from the tools at his feet. He lifted it and swung—and then Mosko let him have it. Three slugs in a row.

Tarelli toppled over next to Rosa. I stepped forward. I don't know what I'd of done next—jumped Mosko, tried to kill him with his own gun. I was in a daze.

Mosko turned around and barked. "Quit staring," he said. "Help me clean up this mess and get rid of them, fast. Or do you wanna get tied in as an accessory for murder?"

That word, "murder"—it stopped me cold. Mosko was right. I'd be in on the deal if they found the bodies. Rosa was dead, Tarelli was dead, the scales and their secret was gone.

So I helped Mosko.

I helped him clean up, and I helped him load the bodies into the car. He didn't ask me to go along with him on the trip, and that was good.

Because it gave me a chance, after he'd gone, to go to the phone and ring up the Sheriff. It gave me a chance to tell the Sheriff and the two deputies the whole story when they came out to the tavern early in the morning. It gave me a chance to see Big Pete Mosko's face when he walked in and found us waiting for him there.

They collared him and accused him and he denied everything. He must of hid the bodies in a good safe place, to pull a front act like that, but he never cracked. He denied everything. My story, the murders, the works.

"Look at him," he told the Sheriff, pointing at me. "He's shakin' like a leaf. Outta his head. Everybody knows he's punchy. Why the guy's off his rocker—spilling a yarn like that! Magic scales that tell your fortune! Ever hear of such a thing? Why that alone ought to show you the guy's slug-nutty"

Funny thing is, I could see him getting to them. The Sheriff and his buddies began to give me a look out of the corner of their eyes.

"First of all," said Mosko, "There never was no such person as Tarelli, and he never had a daughter. Look around—see if you can find anything that looks like we had a fight in here, let alone a double murder. All you'll see is the scales here. The rest this guy made up out of his cracked head."

"About those scales—" the Sheriff began.

Mosko walked over and put his hand on the side of the big glass dial on top of the scales, bold as you please. "Yeah, what about the scales?" he asked. "Look 'em over. Just ordinary scales. See for yourself. Drop a penny, out comes a fortune. Regular stuff. Wait, I'll show you."

We all looked at Mosko as he climbed up on the scales and fumbled in his pocket for a penny. I saw the deputies edge closer to me, just waiting for the payoff.

And I gulped. Because I knew the magic was gone. Tarelli had put the regular works back into the scales and it was just an ordinary weighing machine, now. HONEST WEIGHT, NO SPRINGS. Mosko would dial a fortune and one of the regular printed cards would come out.

We'd hidden the bodies, cleaned up Tarelli's room, removed his clothes, the tools, everything. No evidence left, and nobody would talk except me. And who would believe me, with my crazy guff about a magic scales that told the real future? They'd lock me up in the nut-house, fast, when Mosko got off the scales with his fortune told for a penny.

I heard the click when the penny dropped. The dial behind the glass went up to 297 pounds. Big fat Mosko turned and grinned at all of us. "You see?" he said.

Then it happened. Maybe he was clumsy, maybe there was oil on the platform, maybe there was a ghost and it pushed him. I don't know. All I know is that Mosko slipped, leaned forward to catch himself, and rammed his head against the glass top.

He gurgled once and went down, with a two-foot razor of glass ripping across his throat. As he fell he tried to smile, and one pudgy hand fumbled at the side of the scales, grabbing out the printed slip that told Big Pete Mosko's fortune.

We had to pry that slip out of his hands—pry it out and read the dead mans' future.

Maybe it was just an ordinary scale now, but it told Mosko's fortune, for sure. You figure it out. All I know is what I read, all I know is what Tarelli's scale told Mosko about what was going to happen, and what did happen.

The big white scale stood grinning down on the dead man, and for a minute the cracked and splintered glass sort of fell into a pattern and I had the craziest feeling that I could see Tarelli's face. He was grinning, the scale was grinning, but we didn't grin.

We just pried the little printed slip out of Big Pete Mosko's hand and read his future written there. It was just a single sentence, but it said all there was to be said . . .

"YOU ARE GOING ON A LONG JOURNEY."

TIME TO KILL

By Henry Kuttner

So shining a reputation did Henry Kuttner achieve for himself in the 1940s as a writer of science fiction—performing as brilliantly as Lewis Padgett and Keith Hammond, and on several occasions Lawrence O'Donnell—that the fact that he began his writing career as an author of horror yarns for *Weird Tales* has been shunted aside. Certainly his very first story, "The Graveyard Rats" (*Weird Tales,* March, 1936), is one of the most fearsome stories anyone ever read.

He wrote many tales of supernatural horror, until the much more attractive economic lure of science fiction drew him away. He was instrumental in helping Ray Bradbury break into the horror field, actually writing the last 200 words of "The Candle", the first story of Bradbury's accepted by *Weird Tales* (November, 1942).

When Kuttner's best market for science fiction, Standard Publications Inc., experimented with a magazine of the supernatural, *Strange Stories,* he was a logical contributor, and among his best stories to its pages was "Time to Kill," published in the June, 1940 issue. Europe had been engaged in war since 1939, but the United States had not yet been visited at Pearl Harbor. At quick reading the story seems to be taking place in London during the early ordeal of its bombing, but close observation reveals that this is a never-never war. Yet the war is unimportant, for it is a horror story, and we find a mature, skilled Kuttner who has moved from the unreal background horrors of H. P. Lovecraft to the realm of psychological terror set in familiar surroundings. Kuttner has written a masterful short story, reprinted here for the first time.

TIME TO KILL

By Henry Kuttner

The city waited, in anxiety and terror, for the next bombardment. Already air-fleets and giant guns had brought flaming ruin; streets were littered with broken masonry and glass, though all corpses had been speedily removed. Perfect organization took no risk of plague. Day after day we looked up and saw planes hovering against the blue, watching, watching. Far away the cannon thundered and men with fixed bayonets battled by the light of star-shells and were shot and stabbed and caught on the wire.

For us, behind the lines, in the waiting city, it was far worse. Our nerves jolted, our minds cried out silently in rebellion against the madness of war. Insanity was in the tense air that brought to us the sound of bellowing repercussions and the crash of toppling buildings.

Each night we had a blackout. In the day we crept through the streets fearfully, visiting our razed homes and once-familiar landmarks, wondering when the war would end. Those of us who remembered 1918 felt it might not end till mankind had been destroyed.

But it is not of the war I am writing—that still goes on, very dreadfully—it is of Rudolph Harmon that I wish to speak. Of Harmon, and his strange telepathic power.

I met him first in the partly destroyed office building which some of the homeless had made their headquarters. The first floor was nearly undamaged, and part of the second; the rest was ruin. Families lived in some of the

77

offices, amid salvaged bed-clothing, and, for the lucky ones, army cots. There were pitiful attempts to make the ratholes homelike—a mirror, a carpet, a picture or two on the walls. For the most part, however, we used the building only as a place to sleep and hide. One looks for little more when at any moment the devastating shells may rush down out of the skies.

I was alone, my wife and child dead in the first air-raid. And the office in which I had bestowed my blankets was already occupied by Harmon, a lean, gaunt, nervous fellow of thirty or so with rather bulging eyes and a scrubby mustache. We made an odd pair, for I was short-set, stocky and clean shaven, built more like a wrestler than the physician I had been before our world ended with the undeclared war.

Crises exclude formalities. I entered with my blankets, there was a question, a grunt, and a nod, and after that the two of us lived together amicably enough, though with some disinterest. Now the office had belonged, I think, to an importer, and what happened to him I cannot say. He was probably dead. His desk was still there, and his stenographer's, with a useless lamp on each and a typewriter broken on the floor.

A dictaphone and a transcriber were in the corner, and Harmon, who was a mechanic of sorts, amused himself by trying to repair these. Very luckily, the building had its own power plant in the cellar, and so we could cook and use electric lights whenever we found an unbroken bulb, which was not often. No illumination could be displayed at night, of course. The soldiers were strict about that, at least at first before they were all called to the front. But by that time we had learned the theory of the blackout.

I had little to do with Harmon for a time. Conversation is difficult when nervous strain is so intense and unremitting. We smoked a good deal, drank surprisingly little, and thought entirely too much. Meanwhile the war went on unceasingly.

And day or night we could hear the far, faint rumbling

of the guns, and after dark their flashes beating like heat lightning over the horizon.

It is difficult to describe the atmosphere of the city during those days, which have not yet ended. One's skin becomes unendurably sensitive, as though all the nerve-endings were exposed. One's brain winces from sudden discordant sounds, and there is always the feeling of expectancy, the momentary dread of hearing the shrill scream of displaced air that precedes the explosion. Though we certainly at last, would have welcomed a shell to end the unendurable eternity of waiting, not knowing what to do, seeing no solution and no hope. The mind, balked of the outlet of action, turns inward and devours itself. Spleen, jaundice, ennui—none of us was quite normal.

In fact, such an atmosphere might be calculated to upset or suspend normal laws, not only of habit and thought, but those rooted in unchanging stability. The very earth seemed unfamiliar beneath our feet; it assumed an aspect of alienage, and seemed as though at any time it might change and shudder and disintegrate into chaos. Faces seemed different, and eyes. One had time to analyze them, to realize the mystery in the simplest things, the articulation of a muscle, the ability of the optic nerve, and of all the other senses. I must stress this point, for it is significant in view of what followed.

Harmon repaired his dictaphone and amused himself by dictating into the machine, keeping an audible diary of the days as they went by. There was little enough to record. By day a skeleton army cleared away the corpses and patrolled the city. At night the army was scarcely a squadron, without lights, for the beam even of an electric torch was dangerous. The stratosphere planes and balloons had powerful telescopes, and one by one our own protecting air-force was ordered to the front.

So we waited, doing trivial and foolish things because we needed an outlet for our emotions and thoughts and energies. The nervous strain poured unceasingly into our brains and men and women found various methods of relieving it.

Liquor, sensuality, sudden outbreaks of violence—all these outlets, and others, were undammed.

Week after week went by; still Harmon and I occupied the same room. We grew to hate it. But we never became really friendly; it was not dislike, but indifference. The food supply began to fail, and we shared whatever we could forage. This, too, was merely a matter of convenience and foresight. One day I came in with a few cans of soup, meat, and one of tuna—I remember the latter especially, for it turned out to be bad—and found Harmon seated before the dictaphone transcriber staring at it intently, the earphones clamped over his head. He started when he saw me and hastily turned off the machine.

"Well," I said, throwing down my booty, "we'll eat for a time, anyway. I'm worried about water, though. A guardsman told me the reservoir was bombed."

The news did not affect Harmon perceptibly. He scratched his mustache nervously, and his bulging eyes watched me with an unreadable expression. I went to the window and looked out.

"Two planes," I said. "At the front they're being shot down in droves. There's a new kind of incendiary magnetized bullet—"

"Stanley," Harmon said abruptly. "I wish you'd listen to this record."

"Eh? What—"

"I'm—afraid, a bit," he told me. "It's a dream, a hallucination, or madness. I don't know which. Last night, you see, I dictated something while I was in a trance. At least I wasn't fully conscious, though I wasn't asleep either. You've heard of automatic writing. It was rather like that—automatic speech. Except that I seemed to be dreaming too. I was"—he coughed and looked away—"committing a murder. It wasn't me, though. My mind, my perception, seemed to be in someone else's body. And my voice was giving my thoughts as they went

80

through my brain. It was, well, horrible enough."

"Nerves, perhaps," I said. "Let's hear it."

Harmon gave me the headpiece. I adjusted the phones over my ears, and moved the needle to the beginning of the record. The wax cylinder rotated. I slowed it down a trifle and listened.

At first I heard only an indistinguishable muttering. This changed to disconnected words, and then to a coherent monologue. Harmon watched me closely. His face was rather pale. And, after a time, I understood why.

For on the record were the thoughts of a killer, confused, chaotic, in the beginning:

"Shadows . . . building shadows . . . jagged . . . thrown by the moon. Stay in shadow. They protect. One can hide from the sky . . . the sky presses down, a pall, smothering, crouching. Death ready to leap out of it. But death doesn't leap. If it would, God if it would . . . no, just waiting. Unendurable. Bombs, shells, bloody rain. Something to tear away the blanket on my brain . . . hot, oppressive. I'm calm outwardly. In my brain is seething, raging turmoil. The thoughts beat, beat, in uneven tides . . . this away below the threshold. To break the broken silence. I dare not scream. Don't. Don't. That would rip off the blanket and leave the brain exposed, palpitating . . . stay in the shadows. Slink along the street, dodging the moonlit patches."

For a space, silence, and the scratching of the record. Then the voice resumed:

"My brain moves, turns sickeningly in my skull. Too full of thoughts and fear. Hate. Sorrow. Emotions. What can I do? The front . . . is certain death. Why do I cling to life? The war may end tomorrow. But we can never leave the city. It isn't on earth any more. The air even is changed. It pulses with vibrations of dehumanized emotion. Like electricity beating at the brain. Supercharged brains. Some outlet, some escape.

"Ah, God, something is moving near me, something spawned here where normal laws are transcended, materializing . . . a dog. Small. Leg broken. Its fur is soft.

81

Fur about its throat. . . . My hands are white in the moonlight against black, silken hair. My hands . . . tighten . . . softly, tenderly . . . my fingers are strong; see the tendons stand out. My brain . . . tides of thought are bursting through the blanket that smothers it. There's cold air blowing on my brain. The shadows are jumping toward me. Swooping. Shutting out the horrible sky. I'm in a cave. The shadows guard me. A cold brain, and my fingers filled with ecstatic aching. My hands are releasing the energy that was bottled up in my brain. The dog's dead."

Again the needle scratched softly, rhythmically.

I glanced at Harmon. He made a peremptory gesture. I heard the voice once more:

"Not enough. Not enough energy released. Brain turning, rocking . . . this is the right way, though. But not a dog. Not enough energy released. Not enough. . . . Light on brass buttons. Khaki uniforms. Asleep. A soldier, leaning against a wall, his gun nearly out of reach. He doesn't hear me. His collar is unbuttoned; it's a warm night. The pulse beats under the skin; a blue vein throbs. Can I approach silently? Yes, he doesn't hear. I move the rifle a few feet further away. Now I stand directly in front of the man. My arms lift. The energy is draining out of my brain into my arms. The throbbing in my skull isn't as sickening . . . perhaps this is enough. No. The energy will rush back unless I. . . .

"The shadows poise to leap. Softly, tenderly, my hands tighten about the soldier's throat. Now, now, leap, shadows, guard me, swiftly, volcanically. A thundering torrent floods from my brain, through my arms, into my hands, down to the fingers that release the power. . . . He is dead. His spine cracked almost inaudibly. Let him lie there. Calm, quiet. The sky isn't pressing down anymore. A wind blows cool and refreshing on my bare brain. . . ."

I had reached the end of the record. I turned off the dictaphone, removed the earphones, and swung to face Harmon. He tugged at his mustache, his lips quivering.

"Well?" he asked.

"Subjective," I said. "You're not mad. Nervous hysteria

may cause somnambulism. You walked in your sleep, that's all."

"Yes," he said. "But a soldier was found this morning strangled on the street down by the river."

I fingered the stubble on my chin. "So? There have been coincidences before."

"I went down to see the body," Harmon said, "but it had been taken away. Then I walked around a bit till I saw a dead dog. A black spaniel with a broken leg. I—I—" His eyes protruded even more than usual; he wet his dry lips. "Could *I* have—"

I grinned and touched Harmon's thin arm. "Could you have strangled a husky soldier? Broken his neck? What do you think?"

He looked relieved for a moment, but immediately his brows drew together. "Insanity is supposed to give you abnormal strength."

"Perhaps. But I strongly doubt whether you could strangle a man thus. I was a general practitioner, not a psychiatrist, but I know something about such matters. Besides, how could you go out and kill a soldier while you were dictating a cylinder full?"

"I thought of that," Harmon said. "But I might have been dictating from memory."

"Did you go out last night?"

"I don't remember going out. I went to sleep about nine-thirty. Then suddenly I found myself at the dictaphone, in a sort of trance. When I'd finished talking, everything seemed to go black. I don't know how much later, I woke up completely. I looked at my watch. It was a little after two. You were asleep, but I almost woke you—I needed to talk to someone."

"I'm sorry you didn't," I said.

I went to the window once more, staring unseeingly at a gutted skyscraper across the deserted street, hearing the low drone of a plane high above.

"Can't you figure out any sort of explanation?" Harmon asked.

"I don't know. It isn't a materia medica. It's just an

idea, a pretty fantastic one. If what you dictated was true—"

"Yes?"

"Then you read someone's mind. Telepathy hasn't been proved so far, though experiments have pointed rather conclusively to its possibility. The brain is a mysterious organ, Harmon. There's little really known about it. The pineal gland, for example, is something of an enigma. And the nature of thought itself—well!"

I lit half a cigarette. "Matter and thought are vibration. Vibrations are wave-impulses and can be transmitted under favorable conditions. The conditions here are extraordinary. Mentally we're all rather haywire. It's in the air. Your mind isn't normal, under this strain, and therefore it may be sensitive enough to get in telepathic rapport with some other mind."

Harmon pondered. "But why don't I have this rapport all the time, then? Why just for ten minutes or so last night?"

"The thoughts you got were conceived under tremendous emotional strain. If my theory is correct, this murderer is mad. Superficially he may not show it; I should be surprised if he did. Iron, rigid self-control denied him a more normal mental outlet. He forced himself to restrain the avalanche piling up in his brain. If he'd have got drunk, for example, he'd have been safe. But inhibitions prisoned him till the flood burst into a channel that would normally have been blocked up.

"I have seen murderers psycho-analyzed, Harmon. They didn't want to kill, as a rule. But they were denied other sources of emotional release, or thought they were. Jack the Ripper was such a case. His fear complex led him to butcher women instead of—marrying, for example. If normal channels are blocked, the flood entered abnormal channels."

Harmon held the wax cylinder in his hand. Suddenly he threw it down violently on the floor, where it cracked and shattered.

"You may be right enough," he said, "but there's still

84

something wrong with my mind, eh?"

"I wouldn't say wrong. Nothing that relief from strain can't cure."

"That's easy to get," Harmon said with heavy irony.

We were silent, listening to the low thunder of the great cannon at the front.

The slow days passed wearily. Some left the city, but not many, for starvation waited in the ravaged countryside. In the metropolis one could hope to find food and water, by dint of diligent searching. We were trapped here, bound by invisible fetters. We were the damned. And Harmon suffered and grew haggard under the strain. His eyes were unnaturally bright, his cheeks red and feverish, his lips cracked. A week later there was a recurrence of his telepathic visitation.

I came in one night, bearing a meager supply of food, to find Harmon crouching above the dictaphone waiting for me. His whole gaunt body was trembling, and his face was a white, bearded mask.

"It's happened again," he said. "An hour ago."

Silently I put down my booty and adjusted the earphones. Vague moonlight filtered through the cracked windows now grimy and dirt-smeared. Harmon was a vague shadow as he leaned against the wall, half-hidden amid the gloom.

Once more I heard the eerie voice:

"Walk, walk, walk. Faster. Expend the energy in my brain. But walk warily. Not in the moonlight. Not under the crushing sky, lest it fall. Hear the guns. Each sound adds a charge to the already overcharged currents in my brain. Killing the dog and the soldier wasn't enough. The potential keeps building up again. I need another release. The shadows won't protect me: they flee, slide away, shrink from me, leaving me exposed to the hammer of the sky. I must kill again.

"This building I am passing . . . people sleep here, refugees. And no doors are locked these days. The hall is very dark. In the corner . . . what is it? A black, shapeless bundle. Someone, wrapped in quilts, asleep. An old man. My eyes are accustoming themselves to the gloom. I seem to see very clearly. It's the energy in my brain; light is energy, of course . . . the guns keep hammering. There's a plane going past, I can hear it.

"And here are the shadows following me. They tell me to kill. They'll protect me, guard me . . . the old man wheezes and groans in his sleep. His neck is withered and scrawny. Its texture is scaly with the wrinkles of age, a webwork of tiny wrinkles. I drop on one knee beside him. Silence, vague moonlight from the open door, and the rhythmic movement of breath stirring parchment-yellow skin. And now the energy drains from my brain, and the pounding grows less violent.

"The shadows lean above me, poised to leap. Softly, tenderly, my hands tighten about the old man's throat. Storm of ecstasy! Of relief, flooding, bursting gates that crumble under the onslaught, leaving my brain cold and quite motionless . . . there is only the slight ache in my fingers, sunk in livid flesh. And it is over. He is dead. My brain is free, at peace. The sky is no longer terrifying. The noise of the guns no longer shakes the citadel of my mind. I am relaxed, utterly, joyously. . . ."

The record ended.

"I know what you'll say," Harmon said nervously. "Telepathy. But that doesn't make it any more pleasant for me. There's a mad killer somewhere in the city, and—and—God knows where it may end!"

"Harmon," I said, "Why don't you go into the country? Anywhere. It's not important. A change of atmosphere is the thing."

"Where can I go?" he asked. "We're in hell here. We can't get out of it. The whole land—the entire world, for that matter. . . ." Harmon was silent, brooding. "It's the end. Man's committing suicide. We can't escape. All my relationships, all my ties with life, were cut during the first raid. There's nothing left. I don't know. . . ."

He dropped his head in his hands and massaged his temples. I stood wordlessly contemplating him.

"Why not smash the dictaphone?" I said finally.

Perhaps Harmon thought I intended irony.

"It's easy for you to talk," he snapped angrily. "You're so damned cold-blooded you've got ice-water in your veins. You can't understand how I feel. . . ."

I grunted and turned away, conscious of a hot resentment toward Harmon. I, too, had suffered losses as bad as his own. How dared he assume that because I showed little emotion, I felt nothing underneath? There was a scene I had't let myself recall—the ruins of my house, and the sight that told me I was wifeless and childless.

I forced my thoughts to safer ground. Some things are too horrible to remember.

A fortnight later I came home after midnight, empty-handed. In my stomach was a dull, insistent ache of hunger. The specter of starvation brooded over the city, taking the place of the planes that had vanished days before. We were alone in a world of the dead. Only the noise of the guns, intermittent now, yet somehow more frantically murderous than ever, told us that others besides ourselves were alive.

Before I entered the room where Harmon waited I heard his voice. Or, rather, the voice of the dictaphone. I walked in just as the record ended.

"Hello," Harmon said dully. "It's happened again. No murder this time, though. Listen."

He got up and gave me the earphones. I started the record afresh.

It began abruptly:

"Kill, kill, before the energy tears my brain apart. Two weeks now without any release. Tonight I must find relief or die. Trying to fight down the murder impulse is useless and dangerous. Eventually it gets too strong for me. And tonight it's strong, horribly so. It's dark, very dark. No moon tonight. And there are no shadows. Just the empty sky pressing down. The guns don't sound so often now, but when they do my expectant brain rocks under the impact. I must release this frightful energy within my head.

87

But how, where? People live in this cottage, I think. But the door is locked. A window . . . it slides up easily enough. People don't fear thieves nowadays. Let me light a match. An empty room, I hear the sound of soft breathing."

The record broke off, then resumed swiftly:

"A bedroom. Another match. Its light shows me a bed, two children asleep in it. Eight or ten years old, perhaps. Their throats are soft, white, waiting. I must kill swiftly. I cannot wait. In my head is a surging, thundering maelstrom. It pounds and shatters against the inside of my skull. No shadows to aid me. But the energy is flowing down into my arms. I must bend over the bed, over the child.

"Softly, tenderly, my hands tighten about his throat. . . . Shut up! Shut up! Damn you . . . the other boy is screaming, he's scrambled out of bed, yelling at the top of his lungs. I hear men shouting. Hurrying footsteps. No time now, no time to kill the child. The window's still open. Now I'm in the street. They're following me, bellowing threats. One more minute and I'd have strangled the boy and released the energy. But there wasn't time. Here's an alley. It's dark. And a side street. The pursuers' voices are dying away. I'm losing them. . . . I'm safe now. Safe? God, my brain's ready to explode!"

The record was finished.

I took off the earphones, and turned to face Harmon. In defiance of the air-danger, he had lit an electric lamp, screening it with a handkerchief. He was sitting, now, before the dictating machine, rigid, ignoring me. I started to speak, and, suddenly, paused, watching him.

A tremor shook Harmon's gaunt body. His eyes were dilated. Slowly, automatically, he lifted the speaking-tube of the dictaphone to his lips and pressed the operating button. The needle began to slide over the wax cylinder.

"I can't sand it," Harmon said, in a dead, expressionless voice. "I can't keep the energy pressure under control any longer. My brain is throbbing, pounding, shaking in my skull. I escaped capture, but no risk is too great if it cools my brain. All the energy is back again inside my head. I must kill, swiftly, swiftly!"

There was an outburst of gunfire far away.

But Harmon did not hear it.

"The energy is moving," he went on. "The tides lift it from my brain, down my arms, into the very tips of my fingers. There it waits, ready to leap forth and escape."

Again the guns muttered ominously.

"Crouch, shadows, ready to spring! Leap to guard me! Guard me as I kill! Now—now—*now!*"

Suddenly Harmon gave a high-pitched, wordless shriek. The speaking-tube fell clattering from his lips. He swung around to face me, his eyes widely distended, his face yellow and glistening with sweat. A spasm of terror twisted his lips.

The guns roared.

The shadow fell on Harmon as I moved swiftly.

Softly, tenderly, my hands closed and tightened upon his throat. . . .

ALANNAH

By August Derleth

August Derleth has always had a leaning for the "traditional" ghost story as personified by such famed tales as "The Shadows on the Wall" by Mary E. Wilkins-Freeman, "Seaton's Aunt" by Walter de la Mare, and "The Upper Berth" by F. Marion Crawford. A large percentage of his supernatural stories have taken them as models, though this predeliction has been from personal choice and not limitation, for Derleth's ability to create effectively in the style of any school of writing he chooses, has been amply demonstrated.

"Alannah" is in the manner he prefers, and it is superbly done. It is a horror story, yet he invests it with a touch of sweetness that modifies the impact. "Alannah" is special in another respect. It was one of seventeen stories written within the period of a single month, usually about one story a night, and all published under the pen name of Stephen Grendon. The pen name was derived from that of the narrator in *Evening in Spring,* an autobiographical novel, and therefore actually told by August Derleth. The stories were all written in 1943, and thirteen of them appeared in *Weird Tales,* as did "Alannah" (March, 1945). In fact, a major reason for the pen name was that *Weird Tales* had too many stories under the Derleth name.

Seventeen of the Stephen Grendon stories, including others published in *Arkham Sampler* and *Avon Fantasy*

Reader, were collected under the title of *Mr. George and Other Odd Persons* by Arkham House in 1963. For some reason, the Stephen Grendon stories possess a subtle quality somewhat different than the supernatural stories which appeared under Derleth's name (a fact conceded by the author himself). Perhaps it derives from the special circumstances of the writing. Perhaps the disguise gave the author the illusion of freedom that caused him to drop certain psychological restraints he normally imposed on his writing. Whatever the reason, the reader will find that this "traditional" ghost story is somewhat different.

ALANNAH

By August W. Derleth

I was never one to be hasty in my judgment of others, but I *do* think that Mrs. Stewart might have paid a little more attention to Maurice, she might have given him the kind of affection he needed. Now that everything is over, there can be no harm in setting down what I know about what happened at that house. Mr. Stewart could not have done any more than he did; he had his work, and sometimes he came out from the city pretty tired. Mrs. Stewart was the one. She was that kind of woman—lived for herself too much, and not enough for others. I don't say that a person shouldn't live for himself—but not alone that. My grandmother used to say that it is much better and richer to love than to be loved. I thought of that often about Mrs. Stewart; I always felt that she never knew what it was to love. Yet I wouldn't want to say that she didn't love her son; nobody knows what love is, and love is a great many things to different people. Sometimes love is the most enriching thing in the world, and sometimes it is not; sometimes it is good and wholesome, and sometimes it is possessive and destructive and evil. Sometimes it is strong enough to live after death, and if love lives after it, then surely hunger and terror and all the emotions of man, made

91

strong enough and great enough, live afterward, too.

The Stewarts had taken the house in the Vermont hills when I joined them. That is, they had moved in for that summer, and they had been there for almost a month when I answered their advertisement for a governess. A great many women simply did not want to take positions so far from the city, which meant, really, that they wanted to be in the city, because the Steward house was only about twelve miles from the nearest city, where Mr. Stewart had his law offices, and from which he came home almost every night to work over his briefs. Mrs. Stewart was not the type of woman I would have thought satisfied with such a place; she was one of those women who, because they think always of themselves, are apt to get very lonely if there is not someone before whom they can perform all their little vanities.

I know it sounds as if I were prejudiced against Mrs. Stewart, but I do not think I was. It's only that if she had been a different kind of person, I don't think anything would have happened—at least, things would not have happened as they did there. I ought to say that the very first time I saw the house, I had the feeling that there was something *wrong* about it. I know people will say, "Isn't that just like a woman!" but it is true, just the same. After I got to know Mrs. Stewart I just naturally thought that she was what was wrong about the house. That was a mistake, I know now. Sometimes I wonder if the house was not responsible for some of the things Mrs. Stewart did—or rather, didn't do. I really don't have any prejudice against her, poor woman; she is what she is, just as I am what I am, and Mr. Stewart, is what he is, and Maurice
• • • •

The house was really a beautiful house. It was old, a low two-story stone house, with a charming roof on which the moss grew green. The stone was yellow, but *wet*—actually wet outside; that I thought was due to the brook that flowed past outside, for there was a brook, a real Vermont brook, and if you've ever seen those crystal streams, with their green-blue water, you will know what I mean. The brook came flowing down from the hills, and right in the center of the grounds around the house, though a little off side, beyond the north end and so behind the house, its former owner had built a deep pool, with a fine brick and stone rim curving in an arc toward the brook from both banks; the brook flowed in one end and out the other. And there were trees all along the brook, so that the pool was always shadowed and dark, and one would have thought that there would be fish in plenty there. But, strangely enough, there were fish above the pool in the brook, lying under the grassy banks, and there were fish below, but there was not a fish or a frog or even a water spider in the pool, though lilies grew there, and their green leaves and yellow flowers made the water seem all the blacker, and there was a curious illusion of bottomlessness about it when you looked into the water.

They told me—that is, Mr. Stewart, who interviewed me—that Maurice was a "problem" child, and I came prepared to deal with something like a thoroughly spoiled youngster. Maurice was then five, or a little older, and he was a singularly beautiful child, with his grave blue eyes, which could sometimes be as merry as the blue water of the brook racing over the sunlit sand and the rocks in its course, and curly blond hair, and a sensitive, full-lipped mouth; his skin was fair, with a good color, and he had an innate understanding of neatness. All that first day I kept waiting for him to explode into mischief, but he did nothing of the sort; he was quiet, a little shy, he looked into books—he was precocious for his age, they told me —and he behaved very well. I thought it would come the next day, but it did not, and finally, somewhat mystified, I went to Mrs. Stewart and asked her bluntly in what way Maurice was a "problem" child.

Mrs. Stewart was a dark-eyed, thin-faced woman. She seemed to be always a little remote from the present, but she was very clearly a most passionate type of woman, for she held her husband absolutely, and many times he deferred his better judgment to hers, though he never condoned error. She carried on a great deal of correspondence, and telephoned friends in the city all day long, and what I held and still hold against her was that she never seemed to find much time for Maurice, even if he was her son. When I asked her, she seemed to be annoyed at once, just as if she should not have had the duty of telling me.

"Oh, didn't Wayne tell you?"

"No, Madam, he did not. I expected a lively, mischievous lad, but I have not found Maurice at all mischievous."

"No, if it were only mischief!" she sighed. "But it is something much worse—I suppose the best way it is to tell you that he is endowed with an overabundance of imagination."

I said nothing.

"It is quite distressing for us, but he has fallen into the habit of telling the most bare-faced lies, and Mr. Stewart and I feel that he must be broken of it. It is embarrassing for us all to hear him speak before those of our friends who week-end with us, and the worst of it all is that there is no explanation for it."

"What kind of lies, if I may ask?"

She waved one hand about half-vaguely, half in a gesture of dismissal. "Oh, all kinds of lies, Miss Kerlsen."

I must admit that I have never liked people who tell lies, though one expects a certain amount of it in children. It was a shock to me to hear that Maurice was addicted to lying; somehow, we are always prone to associate goodness and all the virtues with beauty, especially in children; and I resolved that I would do all in my power to break Maurice of prevaricating. The next day I even went so far as to test him. I saw him break a little dish in the kitchen, and carefully pick up the pieces to discard them in the ash-can; so I asked him quite casually about an hour later what had become of the little dish, as if I wanted to see it for something.

"I broke it, Miss Kerlsen," he said candidly.

That puzzled me. I reasoned that if he were the bare-faced liar his mother said he was, he would certainly have lied about the dish; he did not know I had seen him. It was very mystifying, and it grew more so as the days slipped by. Until the sixth day—that was Saturday, for I came on the Monday of that week. That day Maurice came over to where I was resting on the low veranda on the south side of the house and said that Alannah wanted to see me. Though I had never seen Maurice with a playmate, I assumed that Alannah was someone from one of the farms nearby.

"Bring her here," I said.

"Oh, no. You've got to go to her," answered Maurice, and held out his hand confidently.

"Very well," I said, laughing, and took his hand.

He led me around the house quite proudly. I thought his playmate would be out in back, that is, on the up-slope of the hill, but there was no one there. Nevertheless, Maurice led the way straight across the yard; I looked all around quickly, but I could see no one. Then we came to the pool, where Maurice was accustomed to spend long hours dreaming, and Maurice pulled at my hand, and sat down, indicating that I was to sit down, too.

"But where is she?" I asked.

"Do not say anything, please, Miss Kerlsen."

His fair face was flushed with excitement, and I thought his pulse had quickened a little. I put up my hand to touch his forehead, to discover whether he had a fever, but I had barely touched his skin before the most extraordinary thing happened. I felt as if my hand had been brushed aside. The impression was only momentary, it is true, and at the same time Maurice leaned away a little to look into the water; so that in a few seconds I decided that the illusion had been caused by the boy's movement. I looked around to where the woods came down at the far end of the lawn, half-expecting to see a little girl come running out; but there was no sign of anyone. Maurice continued to gaze into the pool, with a little smile on his lips. His eyes, though, were somewhat anxious.

Suddenly, without a word, he stood up, offered me his hand, and hurried me back to the veranda. He smiled quickly at me, and then hastened back around the house. I was astonished by his action, and took the trouble to walk out from the veranda until I could look back into the lawn there to see where he had gone. Just as I suspected, he was sitting on the rim of the pool once more, looking into that dark water, reaching down with one hand.

That evening, as I stood beside his bed, I asked him, "And where was your Alannah this afternoon, Maurice?"

"You didn't see her," he answered in a curiously flat tone of her voice, as if he were disappointed.

"No, I didn't," I answered. "How does she look?"

"Oh, she's pretty."

"Is she as pretty as Mother?"

"Yes."

"Where does she live?"

"In the pool."

So at last I understood what the Stewarts meant by saying that Maurice was a "problem" child, that he told barefaced lies. It was not true that he told lies of all kinds; of that I was certain. He had probably told his parents about Alannah, and they had not understood that a sensitive, imaginative child lives in a world of make-believe, and, lacking companions in the flesh, is very apt to conjure up imaginary companions. At the moment I did not say anything; I only smiled at Maurice, but I was instantly resentful that his parents should not have taken a little more trouble to find out that what Maurice needed more than anything else was companionship. There was no one—only his mother, the cook, an old gardener who came over from a nearby farm, and myself, with his father in the evenings, all far older than the boy—no one his own age. And since there was no likelihood of there being anyone his own age here for the summer, I knew that I would have to enter into his play-world with him as much as possible.

I went right down to where Mr. and Mrs. Stewart sat, in a screened-off porch on the west side of the living room, and asked them whether the boy's imagination was the thing that had caused them to think of him as a problem child.

"It is lies," said Mrs. Stewart stubbornly.

"I would not call them lies," I answered, just as stubbornly. "The boy is just lonely, and he makes up these things."

Mr. Stewart looked up from his papers and observed that it was surely not a healthy sign. He seemed genuinely concerned.

"I don't know what you mean by healthy, but it's certainly normal enough."

"No, no it is not," said Mrs. Stewart.

"That is just not my opinion alone, Mrs. Stewart," I replied.

"I don't care whose opinion it is. Maurice has got to be stopped from telling those—those tall tales or whatever you want to call them." Her eyes flashed at me. "We are depending on you to do what you can."

"I shall do what I can, but I think it is the worst thing in the world to treat the boy as if he were a liar. I will not do that."

"We expect you to do things in your way, Miss Kerlsen," said Mr. Stewart.

The issue, you see, was not cleanly forced. It never was; Mrs. Stewart remained emotional about it, and annoyed; Mr. Stewart was too far from its daily manifestations, obviously. And I—well, I suppose you might say that if I had a more common-sense attitude, I lacked imagination in almost the same proportion as Maurice had an overabundance of it. I suppose if I had had a little more of it, what happened would not have had to happen.

As I was coming up the stairs considerably later that night, I saw Maurice coming down the hall. The hour was almost midnight, though it was a clear night, with a moon shining, and I wondered what he was doing up at that hour. He could have got himself a drink in the bathroom next to his room; but it was not that. I concealed myself and watched him go by. He went down and out of the house, and I went after him, not making a sound.

He went right over to the pool and crouched down on the rim in his white nightgown, and I heard his whispered voice calling, "Alannah! Alannah!" in hushed tones. And then suddenly a little rippling came on the water, a vapor that was not there before. How it startled me! I felt chilled at the sight of it, but it was gone again just as quickly as it had come; there was nothing there, and I began to think my eyes had played a trick on me when Maurice came along with his hand held out and up, just as if he were holding someone's hand, the hand of an older person, and he kept looking up from time to time, as if he were listening to someone walking at his side.

I cannot describe my feelings as I saw that. It was uncanny. I saw him, quite clearly in the moonlight, but there was absolutely nothing else moving across the lawn—only that curly-headed lad in his white nightgown. But when he went past me, where I stood in the shadow of an old tree near the house, I felt his passage as if a cold wind had brushed me, and once again that feeling of unutterable chill, and something of terrible emotional intensity rose up and seemed to cling to me, like something alive; so that I was frightened, almost terrified, by something I could not see or hear, something less tangible than the wind. That feeling lingered until after Maurice had gone into the house, and it was some moments before I could bring myself to follow him.

I went straight to the stairs—he had to go upstairs to his bed—and the moment I put my hand on the stair-rail, I withdrew it as if I had touched ice. I might as well have done so, for the rail was *wet*, wet and *cold*, oh, how cold! And the moment I touched it, I felt the most awful loneliness I ever knew, I felt the most dreadful solitude, as if I were isolated in a place far, far from any human touch or voice, and I felt invaded by the most tearing longing, the most moving desire for someone to hold close to me, someone to possess, *to love!*

It was awful!

I wrenched my hand away and fell back against the wall, shaking and trembling. I put on the light, and, though I would not touch the stair-rail again, I saw the wet gleaming on it all the way up, and I followed it; I saw the wet along the hall and the wall and I saw it on the knob of the door to Maurice's room. I did not want to touch it again, but I had to know that he was all right. So I leaned forward, bracing myself, and quickly opened the door.

The instant I touched the wetness, I felt it again—oh, the most heart-rending despair, the most pitiful agony, the most utter desolation! Oh, the terrible wanting for someone, someone near, someone to love and adore, someone to belong to and to belong to me! I clung to the door and looked in; but he was there, safe in his bed; and I pulled the door shut and drew away from it, shuddering and gasping, for such a tearing emotion I had never known, such a cold isolation of the spirit, such a dread and terror and *emptiness*. It was just as if all the sorrows and griefs of a lifetime had come to life anew and taken away all the memories of compensating pleasures, as if someone were forever doomed to live out his years far from his kind—oh, it is impossible to describe it, it was terrible!

Whatever they may say of me, I am not a coward. I knew then that there was something horribly wrong about the house. Despite the crying out of every instinct against it, I forced myself to go back downstairs, back out across the lawn to the pool. I sat down on the rim, and looked into that black water, where now the moonlight lay like silver, and I could see my face there looking up at me out of that dark, moonlit water, spectrally. It was beautiful there, with the moonlight all around, and the brook talking above and below the pool, and occasionally the sound of a fish splashing. I sat there looking into the pool for five minutes, ten minutes—I do not know what I expected to see there. Certainly it was not what I saw just as I got up to go—that other thin face, a woman's face, with dark where her eyes should have been, and light hair flowing wetly down beside her head, so sharp and strong that I thought it was someone looking over my shoulder into the water, and turned, but then there was nothing in the water either, nothing but my own face looking down. But there was something inside me again—once more that terrible loneliness, that poignant longing, that incredible, hurtful wanting, and agonized desolation which shook me and tore me and sent me staggering away from that pool and brought me to my knees in tears, that strong it was, that terrible and moving.

I fled to the house and was glad to be in my room, myself once more, save for the trembling and the pity I felt for whatever it was in such desperation out there.

I think it was two days later that I found the letter. It was stuck in an old album, put into where a photograph should have been, and left in a closet off my room. It was ten years old, in a man's handwriting, and it was addressed to Mrs. Luella Withers. It was not a nice letter.

Lu Alannah:

I have tried all week to talk myself into coming back and starting over, but it's no use. I'm too weak to do it, I never was much on the noble side of things anyway. So I've taken passage on a tramp steamer for Singapore and the Malay States, which makes it easy for you to get a divorce on grounds of desertion. I want you to have the house; it is really yours, you planned it and all. I am sorry there never was a youngster to share it with us for the little while we were there together. It was rotten luck, but it was our luck.

Jack.

I put it back where I found it and went down to talk to Mrs. Stewart. I asked her who had lived in this house before.

"A Mrs. Luella Withers, Miss Kerlsen."

"What kind of woman was she?"

She shrugged. "I have no idea. She's dead, of course. The house belongs to some relative and we leased it through an agent."

She knew nothing at all about Mrs. Withers. I was half of a mind to point out to her that it was a curious coincidence to discover that Mr. Withers had called his wife by the same pet name that Maurice called his friend. I should not have asked Mrs. Stewart at all; she said she thought it was not "proper" to inquire into the habits and the life of the previous tenant of the house. I should have talked to someone else right away. As it was, it was three days after that before I managed to take a few hours one afternoon while Maurice was asleep to walk down the country road and pay a visit to one of the neighbors.

Mrs. Warren was a farmer's wife, well along in years, but still a big, strong woman. She was canning strawberries that day, and I sat in the kitchen with her, after telling her who I was. Like most country people, once they have no reason to be suspicious of you, she was very friendly with an ease of manner that made it very pleasant to talk to her. She took me for just what I was, and only asked about the Stewarts in the most casual way, not prying at all, but just wanting to know something about her neighbors, so that it was easy for me, at last, to come around to the subject of Mrs. Luella Withers.

"Oh, yes, I knew her," said Mrs. Warren. "Poor, poor woman!" She shook her head, and an expression of sympathy appeared in her warm brown eyes.

"Was she unhappy here?"

"Unhappy's not in it. She was terrible lonesome. I never saw a woman—nor a man, either—that lonesome. She would set and eat her heart out. Her husband got lost on a steamer somewhere. Nobody knows what made him up and take the trip in the first place. They didn't have any children; so she was left alone. And how she wanted a child! I don't know what it was, but I think she was the one couldn't have children. Anyway, if a body took a boy or a girl up along with her visiting there, she never wanted the child to leave, she used to try to keep him there or coax him back—why, it was something awful the way she carried on! They said the lonesomeness just went to her head. It made her thin and hungry-looking, and I reckon in the end it would have killed her."

"She is dead, then?"

"Oh, yes. Couldn't stand it any more. I guess he left her the house, but there wasn't much money; she tried to sell it, but she couldn't; and she couldn't go anywhere else —no money, you see—so one fine day she up and drowned herself."

"In the pool," I said almost involuntarily.

"Yes. They say it's deeper than a body thinks."

It gave me a queer helpless feeling to listen to Mrs. Warren tell about Mrs. Withers. "Tell me," I said at last, "did you ever hear her called *Alannah?*"

"That was *his* name for her. I reckon it's a sweetening name. It's not a name that's in the books, but he would say it the way a man would talk to his sweetheart, and she would smile and her eyes would shine—so I reckon that's what it was."

After that, I felt that the best thing for Maurice would be to get him away from there. I thought it all over that night, and the next morning, before Mrs. Stewart left, I went downstairs and talked to them both at the breakfast table. Maurice was still asleep. I said that I had been thinking everything over, and I felt that Maurice was not lying at all, that his loneliness was responsible for his queer fancies. Perhaps I should have said that I was not sure they were fancies, but I knew that if I had, they would have discounted everything I recommended; so I could not; I had to hold back part of the truth. They were somewhat put out, but I convinced them.

Then I said, "If I make a further suggestion, I would most strongly recommend that Maurice be not told of your intention to leave until it is time to go, or else he may brood about it."

"That is going too far," said Mrs. Stewart. "I will not have the boy growing up a mollycoddle. He will have to learn now that life never gives anybody his way all the time."

I said that the principle was a sound one, but in this case, I felt its application would work adversely, and I begged them to reconsider, with such earnestness that Mr. Stewart said finally they would think it over, and there the matter rested—until the day before they left.

Mrs. Stewart had her way after all. True, they compromised. Mr. Stewart thought I was right, but Mrs. Stewart thought she was right; so they compromised by not telling Maurice until the morning of the day before they planned to return to town, and then they told him.

We were all sitting at the table that morning, and when they told him, I saw his face; he went all white, and one hand clenched tightly around his fork.

"I'm not going," he said in a low voice.

"What was that?" asked Mrs. Stewart.

"I'm not going," he said again.

"I don't think you need more than a day to say goodbye to your *friend*," and Mrs. Stewart coldly.

Mr. Stewart coughed.

Maurice put down his fork precisely and sat back.

"Eat your breakfast, Maurice," said Mrs. Stewart warningly.

"I'm not hungry."

"Eat."

"I won't."

Mrs. Stewart looked up with flashing eyes. "You see, first it is lies and then it is disobedience," she said to no one in particular. "It goes from bad to worse, and if he is this way now, what will he be in a few years from now?"

Maurice got up and went away from the table.

"Come back here!" cried Mrs. Stewart in a voice that was shrill with anger.

Maurice never said a word but simply walked out of the room.

Mrs. Stewart would have got up and gone after him, but he held her back. He said brusquely that telling Maurice had been a shock, and it was better to let it work itself out of him without any unnecessary pressure. I was grateful for that, and Mrs. Stewart, after brooding about Maurice's behavior for a few minutes, resumed her breakfast and grew quite cheerful again, as if she had forgotten the entire incident.

But I did not forget it. I watched Maurice carefully all that day, and I watched him especially at the pool. I was short with his lessons that day because I knew he would want to go around and bid his favorite haunts goodbye. He did not say very much, but I could see that he had something on his mind. People often think, particularly adults who have grown far away from their own childhood, that a child's world is dependent upon the world of the adults;

but this was never so and will never be true, for a child always lives in his own world, no matter what his circumstances, and a sensitive child never completely forgets that world in his adulthood.

I was glad when Maurice fell asleep that night. He had spent a long time at the pool during the late afternoon, and I felt sure that he had been bidding Alannah goodbye; so I asked him gently that evening whether he had.

"Yes. She doesn't want me to go, and I don't want to go. Miss Kerlsen, I like her better than Mum. Is that wrong?"

"I don't think so if you keep it your secret." It was a difficult question to answer.

"Alannah loves me."

"Yes," I said, with a catch in my throat. "Yes. I'm sure she does. But you can come back some time and see her again."

He looked at me gravely and smiled. "They always tell me I'm lying when I talk about Alannah, but you don't, Miss Kerlsen."

"I believe you, Maurice," I said.

"Thank you," he answered.

I did not leave him until he had fallen asleep. And then I sat up until one o'clock in the morning.

As it turned out, I did not sit up long enough. I was very tired, for I had helped with the packing, and I fell asleep. It was about two o'clock when I awoke, and the waning moon had just reached about tree-height in the sky. I do not know what woke me, unless it was the movement of something before my eyes, closed as they were; that is an experience far more usual than is commonly supposed. I had fallen asleep before the window that looked down to the lawn and the brook; the pool lay within easy sight, and the object which had crossed before my eyes was Maurice in his nightgown on his way to the pool.

I was fully awake on the instant. I came out of my chair to my knees at the window and called to him.

"Maurice! Maurice! Come back!"

But he did not turn. He went straight over to the pool and he sat down on the rim of it, and I heard his voice, low

104

and soothing, as if he were comforting someone, and then I saw that vapor again, like a long, white woman's arm come up out of the water and take his hand and pull him into the pool.

I screamed, stumbled to my feet, and ran out of the room as fast as I could—down the stairs and across the lawn.

But I was too late. Maurice had gone under and he did not come up again until he had drowned.

Even while the others came running from the house, there was something else. While I knelt there at that dark pool I felt something come out of it and go past me toward the stone house behind, and I saw the grass move in the moonlight as if two people walked there. And what I felt was not cold, it was not any more that terrible, despairing loneliness—no, it was warm and fulfilling, ineffably beautiful, as if the heart and soul of love itself had become briefly, briefly tangible there and touched me in passing by.

LUANA THE LIVING

By Ray Bradbury

The many years of apprenticeship that Ray Bradbury spent learning his craft before becoming a selling writer has been frequently commented upon, not only by his friends, but also by himself. Estimates of the amount of material he destroyed as unsuitable for publication ranges into millions of words.

One of the reasons he entered the tight circle of science fiction fans in 1937 was that they published amateur magazines which provided an outlet for would-be writers. Yet, though he contributed to many of them, Bradbury's published effort in the late thirties and early forties tended to be more fragments than complete stories, displaying a side to his character literally never found in recent work, that of slapstick humor.

There were a number of exceptions to this predominance of public buffoonery in his amateur efforts. One of them was the psychological fantasy titled "Luana the Living," which appeared in the June, 1940 issue of *Polaris,* a little more than one year before Bradbury sold his first story when he was twenty years of age.

Polaris was a literary publication for its day, edited by a well-liked, serious-minded young man named Paul Freehafer, who was to die of a heart condition in March, 1944. In addition to Ray Bradbury, the magazine ran fiction, poetry, articles and art work by names that are today highly regarded among the fantasy specialists, though some of them have received more universal acclaim. The magazines six "quarterly" issues, published from December, 1939 to June, 1941, ran material by Hannes Bok, Robert W. Lowndes, Duane W. Rimel, R. H. Barlow, Donald A. Wollheim, Damon Knight, Wilson Tucker, Forrest J. Ackerman, John F. Burke, among others.

From its third issue on it was distributed free to the 50 members of The Fantasy Amateur Press Association, and it is extremely doubtful if its total circulation at any time ever exceeded 100 copies.

In a special appreciation to Paul Freehafer, Ray Bradbury wrote in 1944:

> The other night I attended the Philharmonic Auditorium. I looked around to see if I could find Paul Freehafer. I couldn't find him. It was the first time I had been to the Philharmonic and not found Paul somewhere in the audience, he loved the theatre, ballet and music so much. I didn't know of course what I know now. I didn't know that Paul Freehafer wouldn't be coming to the Philharmonic anymore. I only wish I could have seen Paul once more and thanked him for being such a liberal, intelligent man . . . He seemed to have a great wealth of understanding, his knowledge of science and literature was phenomenal . . . Paul had a substantial, unemotional and intelligent approach to fantasy and science-fiction.

"Luana The Living" is of special interest to those who have followed Ray Bradbury's work, since it is one of the few *serious* fantasies that predates his professional work, and is obviously a completed unit, not an experiment or a fragment. He had not yet developed his own style, and literary detectives could enjoy a field day determining influences, but after they are through considering H. P. Lovecraft and Lord Dunsany, they should quickly switch to the "masterpieces" of Wayne Rogers and Hugh B. Cave in *Horror Stories* and *Terror Tales!*

This is the first time "Luana The Living" has ever been reprinted in any form since its initial publication.

LUANA THE LIVING
By Ray Bradbury

Before I conclude this mundane existence, bid the terrors of the alien farewell, and take my leave of all things light and dark, I must tell to someone the reason for my suicide. A horror clings malignantly to my brain, and far back in the recesses of the subconscious it burns like the pale flame of a candle in the tombs of the dead. It steals my strength and leaves me weak and trembling like a child. Try as I will, I can not rid myself of it, for the night of the full Moon forces its return.

I am seated here in the dark, silent room waiting. A few feet distant stands the huge grandfather clock that has been in the family for generations, its gaunt face glowing faintly in the blackness, striking out the hours with a low and gentle tone. The ancient timepiece shall accomplish the action I dare not trust to my shaking hand, for at the last stroke of midnight, fifteen minutes hence, a lever shall press the trigger of the revolver bolted to its side, and send a bullet crashing through my heart. While I wait I shall—I must—unburden myself of my tale.

I am an adventurer, my life not one of common experience. But now, at one score and ten, I am an old man, with silver hair and trembling fingers. Fear has chiseled its effects in my face through sunken eye and wrinkles like those in the skin of a mummy. I am a spent and tired ancient, ready to close my coffin lid down and rest for eternity.

Let me go back a year. Let me seek out the days that

have passed, so short a time away, yet so hellishly removed by the constant torture that has made twelve months seem like a century.

In India, back along the mountainous spine of the Himalayas, in a dark region where tigers prowled, I had been deserted by my natives who had babbled of some superstitious legend about "Luana." As I broke my way through a thick wall of brambles, I came across a hirsute individual who squatted cross-legged beneath a tree, puffing gently on his opium pipe. Hoping to gain a guide, I accosted him, but received no answer.

I looked into his eyes, small almond holes in the midst of converging wrinkles, and saw no iris or pupil, just a small expanse of leaden flesh as if the eyeballs had been rolled back in hypnotic sleep by the opium. And he said no word, but swung gently from side to side like a sapling in the summer wind, spurts of smoke blowing from his lips. In a rage at his silence, I shook him until the pipe fell from his mouth. His jaw sprang down and his lips curled back revealing a row of sharp, yellow teeth. My stomach revolted at what I saw. He could not talk, this stranger, for his tongue was blue and shriveled like a dried fig which someone had slit open, its blood withdrawn. A dreamlike gibberish issued from far in his throat and I let him loose. Immediately the hands fumbled about on the ground, recovered the pipe, and replaced it in the mouth. He continued his tranquil puffing, blind and speechless, and I withdrew from the vicinity in haste.

For the remainder of the day I cut my way through jungle never explored by white man. Perishing from thirst and hunger, I tried unsuccessfully to follow barely discernible animal paths to a water hole. When I tried to return to the point where I had hacked my way through the bramble barrier, both my path and the strange blind man had vanished. It was almost as if the brambles had grown together in the few scant hours. And when I saw the cut I had made in a tree earlier, I realized the brambles had grown, for the cut had moved upward visibly. This was a land of insanely growing jungle, where plants sprouted, grew, and died in a week or two. The carpet of vegetation was feet thick and strangely resilient, and the unpleasant jungle was hot and broad and quiet. Not even the bestial cry of a tiger broke the oppressive silence, which pressed its fingers in upon me until I shouted to please my ears, to shock myself back into sanity. When I could no longer stand the strange lack of noise, I would run through brush and mire, slipping and falling and sliding until I was bathed in perspiration, then I would sit and rest and watch the mud on my shoes dry and form into crooked cakes.

And still no sound. There was some grim thing that fettered this tree-bounded terrain in soundless monotony.

As the sun floated briefly on the ocean of leaves and branches and vanished in the West, I realized that this was a place apart, undisturbed by the outer world which it repulsed by its wall of thorns. There were few water holes and animals in the land of silence, and the natives were furtive and rarely seen. I dimly recalled strange tales of them and this region, about practices that took place in the light of the full Moon.

As twilight came the cavern of space sprouted points of light that were the stars. Hours passed and the hushed night became sprinkled with more and more of the silver points until a veritable blanket of light diffused the dome of heaven. As I sat and gazed upward through the trees toward them, I sensed a movement about me. It seemed that the whole forest was stirring to life. Little leaves slithered under foot, slender saplings wavered and shook, and the mighty jungle giants themselves bestirred and fluttered their leaves to the ground. In the dark it seemed that things grew threefold the speed of daylight, shot up and bloomed by some mysterious means. The trees broke the silence with a faint rustling and the underbrush writhed with evil life. I arose and moved on as through a bog, the rot under foot hindering me until I fell forward and sprawled with my face in the soil.

Suddenly as I lay there, it seemed that tendrils swept up and clung to me, caressed my neck in an unrelenting grip until I strangled and gasped for air. Knotted vines wrapped swiftly on my forehead and pressed my temples until a stabbing pain flickered through me. I tore at my throat, freeing it with feeble gestures of the clutching things, and staggered to my feet. Desperately I stumbled on, until my foot struck water unexpectedly, and I ventured forward until the chill liquid reached my knees.

My terrors was forgotten as I dropped to my knees in the scummy water and brushed aside the web-like debris. Ripples quivered under hand, and as I bent I saw the stars reflected in its surface like dancing fireflies. I gulped in huge mouthfuls and wetted my forehead and my temples to ease the heated pain that dwelt there. Then I lay back and floated in the pool, watching the water caress my tattered boots and puttees.

How long I lay and relaxed I know not. When I emerged, dripping, I had found a new strength that grew by the minute. I stripped the torn shirt from me and soaked it in the water, then twisted it and tied it about my head so that its moisture would keep me comfortable for a while. The water clung to my skin, shimmering like a grayish slime.

Intrigued by the dark now, my terror vanished, and I moved forward among the leaping tendrils. Tiny rustlings, the secretive murmuring of water and soil, the high-pitched crackle of branches sounded and the jungle was a living, breathing creature that I walked upon. Then before me I could see a clearing where dark shapes poised in a circle in its gloomy depth.

I stopped suddenly, as if frozen by a sudden blast of wintry wind. I squinted at the shapes crouching on the ground in the clearing. It seemed that I saw a double score of stone statues imbedded in the soil, squatting and waiting, malignant. In the center crouched another presence, alone on the sodden surface.

A light flecked the tree tops a moment later. As the seconds passed by the full sphere of the Moon ascended the star-sprinkled vault inch by inch. It saturated the clearing with silver and brought forth the crouching

111

shapes like silhouettes on the jungle floor.

Something moved. A figure shifted, and realization of what I saw came to me. These were men! Men, waking as if from sleep, one by one. A soft soughing sound as of wind stirring through myriads of leaves arose as the Moon ascended. I advanced slowly, quietly, toward the clearing. The creatures on the ground stretched long, thin limbs, and knelt upon their knees, all bowing toward the Moon in the crystal-clear sky, all with their emaciated backs toward me.

They seemed creatures of some hypnotic spell, their movements drug-like, as they raised their fingers and gesticulated toward the lunar world that swung from the trees, a disc of blinding white. It was a scene painted in platinum. The Moon dominated the sky and the stars paled to insignificance in its white fire. Now the members of the cult arose and swayed from side to side, swinging their hands and lamenting with deep-chested sounds.

They swung about swiftly, undulated and leaped and danced, the ground throbbing under their bare feet. In a circle they moved, hurtling up and slapping their palms together and weeping. They chanted and screamed and beat their bodies and swept by me without seeing. Like gnarled trees sprung to life they move, naked and brown. But it was their eyes that caused me to fear. For they were leaden and white without pupils, as if burned to that sickly colour by exposure to some changing light, as if dyed by the light of the Moon!

One man, standing in the center of the racing throng, stood and motioned to the Moon, and I recognized him as the stranger I had accosted that morn, the man with the shrunken tongue and blind eyes! He was gibbering and urging his comrades on, and strangely his words became gradually understandable in the tongue of the ancient Hindus.

"Great living Luana! Give us strength, Protect us! Keep from us the unholy spirit of the white man! Destroy the ulcer of the earth, all mankind, those who poison the true faith with their ignorance!"

Overcome with anger, I foolishly stepped into their midst with my revolver in my hand, and commanded them to stop their ritual. They stopped as if struck by lightning! But only for a moment. Then with cries of bestial rage they advanced toward me, imploring the Moon as it hung full suspended above the trees.

"Destroy this invader! Annihilate the ignoble savage who has seen the ritual of Luana!" they pleaded. "Luana lives and breathes! Luana, take revenge for us who are blind yet see your light." I leveled my revolver, praying that the water had not wetted the powder, and fired point blank into one savage heart. With a curse on his lips the man stumbled and fell, throwing me to the ground. From where I lay I saw the others scatter wildly, weaving and vanishing into the jungle. I fired and kept firing until the hammer of my gun clicked harmlessl. Then I glared about and saw the last native kneeling on the ground and praying.

"I curse this man in the name of living Luana," he sighed. Without another word he sank upon the sward and lay deathly still.

If I had but known the consequences of my action! A fountain of light spurted down as I let my weapon drop, and I looked full into the face of the Moon and gasped. It seemed that it filled the sky with its bulk, flamed with a radiance brighter than the sun, battered me and burned my eyes with its intensity. A wrathful, malignant sphere wavered over me as an evil god, and it seemed that the Moon lived and breathed as did the jungle. It was as though this jungle were the Moon's abode, these natives its disciples in some weird cult.

I remember screaming once, a half-hearted scream of unbelief, and then I ran! Tearing away branches and slogging through marshy ground, I reached the bramble barrier and raised my knife to hack away the thorns. A sudden dizziness whirled over me and I sank down into oblivion. The last thing I viewed was the pulsating pockmarked face of Luana glimmering hot on my eyes.

The next morning I found myself outside the bramble

wall on a familiar trail. My gun was gone and my knife had vanished also, but my mind made itself believe that all had been a nightmare. God, if only it had been!

I returned to civilization immediately, and, chartering a special plane, reached America within the next twenty days. At home, here in the country, overlooking the California coast and the Pacific Ocean, I rested for a few days. But on the night of the next full Moon—

I could no longer sit upon my veranda. A vague warning issued from the vaults of the cratered Moon itself, and squat alien figures seemed to crouch in the shade of the myriad trees. A sibilant and throbbing song like gushing blood echoed and pounded in my ears. My friends left me alone to my musings because of the fear I displayed and an almost fanatical haste to escape the light of the Moon as it dangled, a crescent of unfilled light, in the heavens. The world had left me to my dreaming, my dreadful nightmares, and the errors that assail me.

Of nights I sat bolt upright and quaked to see the moon in all its odious whiteness cling upon the curtain of night to bathe my chamber in platinum. So frightened I became that I summoned a maker of tapestries and instructed him to hang upon the windows curtains of ebon color to shut out forever that pale and sickly-hued torrent of luminescence.

But even though the shades were drawn and the curtains clamped tight, I heard the mourning of wind about the trees like the high-pitched mourning of those devil savages, stirring shadow creatures to life under the spell of earth's satellite. And, growing from full Moon to full Moon, I have heard other sounds, sounds of bestial activity springing up among the shrubs, as if those growths had been stung to live and they cracked and shook with warning. Leaves crunched brittlely on the trees and tore away to flutter impatiently on the sill of my retreat. Noises—noises that confounded and worried me—that urged me to desperation until clammy sweat broke out upon my brow.

And then, twelve moons from that night in the jungle, I

lay in the humid room in the dark, bathed in moisture, waiting for some cool breeze to bring me the sleep that I prayed for. A solid wave of heat crawled over me until all rational thought had fled and I was crazed for a breath of fresh air. I staggered to the curtains, shut my eyes tightly so as not to perceive the Moon in all its somberness. I swept aside the shrouds and threw open the tall window, sucking in my breath, waiting to quaff the chilly night. Instead, a river of noise and a wind born of fire struck me fearfully. The wind harked louder and tore my remaining garments from me as I stood in its beating flames, swept around and burnt as if by some equatorial daylight.

I clutched at the windows, seeking to shut them again, seeking to close off the chatter of leaves and wind and shadows, leaping with evil life. A noise like laughter descended from above, a song of hate from blasphemed Nature; chant of sea and aria of birds, trilling of zephyrs and thunder of tornado, mingled in a rising clangor which hammered at me. Fire burned through me, scorched open my eyes and made me lift my lids to view the Moon where it lay in rafters of clouds. Like some god, titanic and wrathful, silver, its surface boiling like a cauldron, it drowned the sky in bulk and stabbed its colorless disc into my brain. The tempest was a continuous straining to break my ear drums.

Somehow I closed the window, shut out the noise, pulled the curtains tight, and no longer saw the light.

I remember moving dazedly back to my dressing table and standing before my mirror as I switched on the light.

That was a fortnight ago.

The time draws near for the clock to strike twelve, as I sit and write these last few words. In one minute, as the clock strikes out the last note, I shall die.

For a fortnight I have been in this room, never venturing out though I am parched with thirst and hollow with hunger. I have not dared to venture forth.

I am committing suicide because—

Ah, the clock strikes twelve. One! Two! Three! . . .

I am killing myself because when I turned on the light in

my room and looked at myself in the mirror, I saw—
Through a grey film that clouded my eyes I saw a gaping
idiot, eyes leaden and white without pupils, face dead and
thin, mouth dropped open, and my tongue—was a
shriveled black mass lolling between my teeth like a
twisted rag.

I bid you farewell! The clock tolls twelve!
                                            -THE END-

JOHN BARRINGTON COWLES

By A. Conan Doyle

Before A. Conan Doyle was on his way to fame and fortune as author of the Sherlock Holmes stories, he had been writing and selling fiction for many years, some of it distinctly fantastic and supernatural. Of course he scored a tremendous success with Sherlock Holmes in *The Strand Magazine* in the early nineties, and contributed outstanding historical fiction to *The Idler* during the same period. But while he was still trying to make his way as a physician, he managed to survive on the proceeds of some short stories published in obscure magazines. Many of these publications are forgotten today, such as *Cornhill, Temple Bar, Belgravia, London Society, Cassell's* and the juvenile *The Boy's Own Paper*, but they had been among his most reliable markets. After the publication of a chronicle-like 17th century historical titled "Micha Clarke," which received good notices and good sale, Longmans, Green, and Co. had collected some of his earlier short stories under the title of *The Captain of The Polestar And Other Tales*, published in 1894. Among those stories was the remarkable work with the unprepossessing title of "John Barrington Cowles."

The story deals with a woman who brings disaster to three men who fall in love with her. The fate that is meted out to them, usually ending in death by apparent suicide, is the result of something she *tells* them about herself. The knowledge is so psychologically untenable, that even though they continue to love her, none of the men can willingly desire to live once knowing it.

The narrator follows the courtship of each of these men and their reaction once they have learned her terrible secret. He finally confronts the woman, but she bluntly informs him that a horrible fate awaits him if he attempts to pry too closely.

The drama continues inexorably, and Doyle builds with magnificent indirection. The unknown horror of what this woman has to impart is never revealed, and the narrator is helpless to stop her, but he presents the story as a warning to others.

The reader is left to surmise with morbid fascination on the nature of this woman and her strange powers, and Doyle has created a masterpiece of horror which, despite his monumental reputation, has remained submerged, virtually unknown and uncommented upon.

JOHN BARRINGTON COWLES

By A. Conan Doyle

PART I.

It might seem rash of me to say that I ascribe the death of my poor friend, John Barrington Cowles, to any preternatural agency. I am aware that in the present state of public feeling a chain of evidence would require to be strong indeed before the possibility of such a conclusion could be admitted.

I shall therefore merely state the circumstances which led up to this sad event as concisely and as plainly as I can, and leave every reader to draw his own deductions. Perhaps there may be some one who can throw light upon what is dark to me.

I first met Barrington Cowles when I went up to Edinburgh University to take out medical classes there. My landlady in Northumberland Street had a large house, and, being a widow without children, she gained a livelihood by providing accommodation for several students.

Barrington Cowles happened to have taken a bedroom upon the same floor as mine, and when we came to know each other better we shared a small sitting-room, in which we took our meals. In this manner we originated a friendship which was unmarred by the slightest disagreement up to the day of his death.

Cowles' father was the colonel of a Sikh regiment and had remained in India for many years. He allowed his son a handsome income, but seldom gave any other sign of parental affection—writing irregularly and briefly.

My friend, who had himself been born in India, and whose whole disposition was an ardent tropical one, was much hurt by this neglect. His mother was dead, and he had no other relation in the world to supply the blank.

Thus he came in time to concentrate all his affection upon me, and to confide in me in a manner which is rare among men. Even when a stronger and deeper passion came upon him, it never infringed upon the old tenderness between us.

Cowles was a tall, slim young fellow, with an olive, Velasquez-like face, and dark, tender eyes. I have seldom seen a man who was more likely to excite a woman's interest, or to captivate her imagination. His expression was, as a rule, dreamy, and even languid; but if in conversation a subject arose which interested him he would be all animation in a moment. On such occasions his colour would heighten, his eyes gleam, and he could speak with an eloquence which would carry his audience with him.

In spite of these natural advantages he led a solitary life, avoiding female society, and reading with great diligence. He was one of the foremost men of his year, taking the senior medal for anatomy, and the Neil Arnott prize for physics.

How well I can recollect the first time we met her! Often and often I have recalled the circumstances, and tried to rememeber what the exact impression was which she produced on my mind at the time. After we came to know her my judgment was warped, so that I am curious to recollect what my unbiased instincts were. It is hard, however, to eliminate the feelings which reason or prejudice afterwards raised in me.

It was at the opening of the Royal Scottish Academy in the spring of 1879. My poor friend was passionately attached to art in every form, and a pleasing chord in music or a delicate effect upon canvas would give exquisite pleasure to his highly-strung nature. We had gone together to see the pictures, and were standing in the grand central *salon,* when I noticed an extremely beautiful woman standing at the other side of the room. In my whole life I have never seen such a classically perfect countenance. It was the real Greek type—the forehead broad, very low, and as white as marble, with a cloudlet of delicate locks wreathing round it, the nose straight and clean cut, the lips inclined to thinness, the chin and lower jaw beautifully rounded off, and yet sufficiently developed to promise unusual strength of character.

But those eyes—those wonderful eyes! If I could but give some faint idea of their varying moods, their steely hardness, their feminine softness, their power of command, their penetrating intensity suddenly melting away into an expression of womanly weakness—but I am speaking now of future impressions!

There was a tall, yellow-haired young man with this lady, whom I at once recognised as a law student with whom I had a slight acquaintance.

Archibald Reeves—for that was his name—was a dashing, handsome young fellow, and had at one time been a ringleader in every university escapade; but of late I had seen little of him, and the report was that he was engaged to be married. His companion was, then, I presumed, his *fiancée.* I seated myself upon the velvet settee in the centre of the room, and furtively watched the couple from behind my catalogue.

The more I looked at her the more her beauty grew upon me. She was somewhat short in stature, it is true; but her figure was perfection, and she bore herself in such a fashion that it was only by actual comparison that one would have known her to be under medium height.

As I kept my eyes upon them, Reeves was called away for some reason, and the young lady was left alone. Turning her back to the pictures, she passed the time until the return of her escort in taking a deliberate survey of the company, without paying the least heed to the fact that a dozen pair of eyes, attracted by her elegance and beauty, were bent curiously upon her. With one of her hands holding the red silk cord which railed off the pictures, she stood languidly moving her eyes from face to face with as little self-consciousness as if she were looking at the canvas creatures behind her. Suddenly, as I watched her, I saw her gaze become fixed, and, as it were, intense. I followed the direction of her looks, wondering what could have attracted her so strongly.

John Barrington Cowles was standing before a picture—one, I think, by Noel Paton—I know that the subject was a noble and ethereal one. His profile was turned towards us, and never have I seen him to such advantage. I have said that he was a strikingly handsome man, but at that moment he looked absolutely magnificient. It was evident that he had momentarily forgotten his surroundings, and that his whole soul was in sympathy with the picture before him. His eyes sparkled, and a dusky pink shone through his clear olive cheeks. She continued to watch him fixedly, with a look of interest upon her face, until he came out of his reverie with a start, and turned abruptly round, so that his gaze met hers. She glanced away at once, but his eyes remained fixed upon her for some moments. The picture was forgotten already, and his soul had come down to earth once more.

We caught sight of her once or twice before we left, and each time I noticed my friend look after her. He made no remark, however, until we got out into the open air, and were walking arm-in-arm along Princes Street.

"Did you notice that beautiful woman, in the dark dress, with the white fur?" he asked.

"Yes, I saw her," I answered.

121

"Do you know her?" he asked eagerly. "Have you any idea who she is?"

"I don't know her personally," I replied. "But I have no doubt I could find out all about her, for I believe she is engaged to young Archie Reeves, and he and I have a lot of mutual friends."

"Engaged!" ejaculated Cowles.

"Why, my dear boy," I said, laughing. "you don't mean to say you are so susceptible that the fact that a girl to whom you never spoke in your life is engaged is enough to upset you?"

"Well, not exactly to upset me," he answered, forcing a laugh. "But I don't mind telling you, Armitage, that I never was so taken by any one in my life. It wasn't the mere beauty of the face—though that was perfect enough—but it was the character and the intellect upon it. I hope, if she is engaged, that it is to some man who will be worthy of her."

"Why," I remarked, "you speak quite feelingly. It is a clear case of love at first sight, Jack. However, to put your perturbed spirit at rest, I'll make a point of finding out all about her whenever I meet any fellow who is likely to know."

Barrington Cowles thanked me, and the conversation drifted off into other channels. For several days neither of us made any allusion to the subject, though my companion was perhaps a little more dreamy and distraught than usual. The incident had almost vanished from my remembrance, when one day young Brodie, who is a second cousin of mine, came up to me on the university steps with the face of a bearer of tidings.

"I say," he began, "you know Reeves, don't you?"

"Yes. What of him?"

"His engagement is off."

"Off," I cried. "Why, I only learned the other day that it was on."

"Oh, yes—it's all off. His brother told me so. Deucedly mean of Reeves, you know, if he has backed out of it, for she was an uncommonly nice girl."

"I've seen her," I said; "but I don't know her name."

"She is a Miss Northcott, and lives with an old aunt of hers in Abercrombie Place. Nobody knows anything about her people, or where she comes from. Anyhow, she is about the most unlucky girl in the world, poor soul!"

"Why unlucky?"

"Well, you know, this was her second engagement," said young Brodie, who had a marvellous knack of knowing everything about everybody. "She was engaged to Prescott—William Prescott, who died. That was a very sad affair. The wedding day was fixed, and the whole thing looked as straight as a die when the smash came."

"What smash?" I asked, with some dim recollection of the circumstances.

"Why, Prescott's death. He came to Abercrombie Place one night, and stayed very late. No one knows exactly when he left, but about one in the morning a fellow who knew him met him walking rapidly in the direction of the Queen's Park. He bade him good night, but Prescott hurried on without heeding him, and that was the last time he was ever seen alive. Three days afterwards his body was found floating in St. Margaret's Loch, under St. Anthony's Chapel. No one could ever understand it, but of course the verdict brought it in as temporary insanity."

"It was very strange," I remarked.

"Yes, and deucedly rough on the poor girl," said Brodie. "Now that this other blow has come it will quite crush her. So gentle and ladylike she is too!"

"You know her personally, then!" I asked.

"Oh, yes, I know her. I have met her several times. I could easily manage that you should be introduced to her."

"Well," I answered, "it's not so much for my own sake as for a friend of mine. However, I don't suppose she will go out much for some little time after this. When she does I will take advantage of your offer."

We shook hands on this, and I thought no more of the matter for some time.

The next incident which I have to relate as bearing at all

upon the question of Miss Northcott is an unpleasant one. Yet I must detail it as accurately as possible, since it may throw some light upon the sequel. One cold night, several months after the conversation with my second cousin which I have quoted above, I was walking down one of the lowest streets in the city on my way back from a case which I had been attending. It was very late, and I was picking my way among the dirty loungers who were clustering round the doors of a great gin-palace, when a man staggered out from among them, and held out his hand to me with a drunken leer. The gaslight fell full upon his face, and, to my intense astonishment, I recognized in the degraded creature before me my former acquaintance, young Archibald Reeves, who had once been famous as one of the most dressy and particular men in the whole college. I was so utterly surprised that for a moment I almost doubted the evidence of my own senses; but there was no mistaking those features, which, though bloated with drink, still retained something of their former comeliness. I was determined to rescue him, for one night at least, from the company into which he had fallen.

"Holloa, Reeves!" I said. "Come along with me. I'm going in your direction."

He muttered some incoherent apology for his condition, and took my arm. As I supported him towards his lodgings I could see that he was not only suffering from the effects of a recent debauch, but that a long course of intemperance had affected his nerves and his brain. His hand when I touched it was dry and feverish, and he started from every shadow which fell upon the pavement. He rambled in his speech, too, in a manner which suggested the delirium of disease rather than the talk of a drunkard.

When I got him to his lodgings I partially undressed him and laid him upon his bed. His pulse at this time was very high, and he was evidently extremely feverish. He seemed to have sunk into a doze; and I was about to steal out of the room to warn his landlady of his condition, when he started up and caught me by the sleeve of my coat.

"Don't go!" he cried. "I feel better when you are here. I am safe from her then."

"From her!" I said. "From whom?"

"Her! her!" he answered peevishly. "Ah! you don't know her. She is the devil! Beautiful—beautiful; but the devil!"

"You are feverish and excited," I said. "Try and get a little sleep. You will wake better."

"Sleep!" he groaned. "How am I to sleep when I see her sitting down yonder at the foot of the bed with her great eyes watching and watching hour after hour? I tell you it saps all the strength and manhood out of me. That's what makes me drink. God help me—I'm half drunk now!"

"You are very ill," I said, putting some vinegar to his temples; "and you are delirious. You don't know what you say."

"Yes I do," he interrupted sharply, looking up at me. "I know very well what I say. I brought it upon myself. It is my own choice. But I couldn't—no, by heaven, I couldn't—accept the alternative. I couldn't keep my faith to her. It was more than man could do."

I sat by the side of the bed, holding one of his burning hands in mine, and wondering over his strange words. He lay still for some time, and then, raising his eyes to me, said in a most plaintive voice—

"Why did she not give me warning sooner? Why did she wait until I had learned to love her so?"

He repeated this question several times, rolling his feverish head from side to side, and then he dropped into a troubled sleep. I crept out of the room, and, having seen that he would be properly cared for, left the house. His words, however, rang in my ears for days afterwards, and assumed a deeper significance when taken with what was to come.

My friend, Barrington Cowles, had been away for his summer holidays, and I had heard nothing of him for several months. When the winter session came on, however, I received a telegram from him, asking me to secure the old rooms in Northumberland Street for him, and telling me the train by which he would arrive. I went down to meet him, and was delighted to find him looking wonderfully hearty and well.

"By the way," he said suddenly, that night, as we sat in our chairs by the fire, talking over the events of the holidays, "you have never congratulated me yet!"

"On what, my boy?" I asked.

"What! Do you mean to say you have not heard of my engagement?"

"Engagement! No!" I answered. "However, I am delighted to hear it, and congratulate you with all my heart."

"I wonder it didn't come to your ears," he said. "It was the queerest thing. You remember that girl whom we both admired so much at the Academy?"

"What!" I cried, with a vague feeling of apprehension at my heart. "You don't mean to say that you are engaged to her?"

"I thought you would be surprised," he answered. "When I was staying with an old aunt of mine in Peterhead, in Aberdeenshire, the Northcotts happened to come there on a visit, and as we had mutual friends we soon met. I found out that it was a false alarm about her being engaged, and the—well, you know what it is when you are thrown into the society of such a girl in a place like Peterhead. Not, mind you," he added, "that I consider I did a foolish or hasty thing. I have never regretted it a moment. The more I know Kate the more I admire her and love her. However, you must be introduced to her, and then you will form your own opinion."

I expressed my pleasure at the prospect, and endeavoured to speak as lightly as I could to Cowles upon the subject, but I felt depressed and anxious at heart. The words of Reeves and the unhappy fate of young Prescott recurred to my recollection, and though I could assign no tangible reason for it, a vague, dim fear and distrust of the woman took possession of me. It may be that this was foolish prejudice and superstition upon my part, and that I involuntarily contorted her future doings and sayings to fit into some half-formed wild theory of my own. This has been suggested to me by others as an explanation of my narrative. They are welcome to their opinion if they can reconcile it with the facts which I have to tell.

I went round with my friend a few days afterwards to call upon Miss Northcott. I remember that, as we went down Abercrombie Place, our attention was attracted by the shrill yelping of a dog—which noise proved eventually to come from the house to which we were bound. We were shown upstairs, where I was introduced to old Mrs. Merton, Miss Northcott's aunt, and to the young lady herself. She looked as beautiful as ever, and I could not wonder at my friend's infatuation. Her face was a little more flushed than usual, and she held in her hand a heavy dog-whip, with which she had been chastising a small Scotch terrier, whose cries we had heard in the street. The poor brute was cringing up against the wall, whining piteously, and evidently completely cowed.

"So Kate," said my friend, after we had taken our seats, "you have been falling out with Carlo again."

"Only a very little quarrel this time," she said, smiling charmingly. "He is a dear, good old fellow, but he needs correction now and then." Then, turning to me, "We all do that, Mr. Armitage, don't we? What a capital thing if, instead of receiving a collective punishment at the end of our lives, we were to have one at once, as the dogs do, when we did anything wicked. It would make us more careful, wouldn't it?"

I acknowledged that it would.

"Supposing that every time a man misbehaved himself a gigantic hand were to seize him, and he were lashed with a whip until he fainted"—she clenched her white fingers as she spoke, and cut out viciously with the dog-whip—"it would do more to keep him good than any number of high-minded theories of morality."

"Why, Kate," said my friend, "you are quite savage to day."

"No, Jack," she laughed. "I'm only propounding a theory for Mr. Armitage's consideration."

The two began to chat together about some Aberdeenshire reminiscence, and I had time to observe Mrs. Merton, who had remained silent during our short conversation. She was a very strange-looking old lady. What attracted attention most in her appearance was the utter want of colour which she exhibited. Her hair was snow-white, and her face extremely pale. Her lips were bloodless, and even her eyes were of such a light tinge of blue that they hardly relieved the general pallor. Her dress was a grey silk, which harmonized with her general appearance. She had a peculiar expression of countenance, which I was unable at the moment to refer to its proper cause.

She was working at some old-fashioned piece of ornamental needlework, and as she moved her arms her dress gave forth a dry, melancholy rustling, like the sound of leaves in the autumn. There was something mournful and depressing in the sight of her. I moved my chair a little nearer, and asked her how she liked Edinburgh, and whether she had been there long.

When I spoke to her she started and looked up at me with a scared look on her face. Then I saw in a moment what the expression was which I had observed there. It was one of fear—intense and overpowering fear. It was so marked that I could have staked my life on the woman before me having at some period of her life been subjected to some terrible experience or dreadful misfortune.

"Oh, yes, I like it," she said, in a soft, timid voice; "and we have been here long—that is, not very long. We move about a great deal." She spoke with hesitation, as if afraid to committing herself.

"You are a native of Scotland, I presume?" I said.

"No—that is, not entirely. We are not natives of any place. We are cosmopolitan, you know." She glanced round in the direction of Miss Northcott as she spoke, but the two were still chatting together near the window. Then she suddenly bent forward to me, with a look of intense earnestness upon her face, and said—

"Don't talk to me any more, please. She does not like it,

128

and I shall suffer for it afterwards. Please, don't do it."

I was about to ask her the reason for this strange request, but when she saw I was going to address her, she rose and walked slowly out of the room. As she did so I perceived that the lovers had ceased to tak., and that Miss Northcott was looking at me with her keen, grey eyes.

"You must excuse my aunt, Mr. Armitage," she said; "she is old, and easily fatigued. Come over and look at my album."

We spent some time examining the portraits. Miss Northcott's father and mother were apparently ordinary mortals enough, and I could not detect in either of them any traces of the character which showed itself in their daughter's face. There was one old daguerreotype, however, which arrested my attention. It represented a man of about the age of forty, and strikingly handsome. He was clean shaven, and extraordinary power was expressed upon his prominent lower jaw and firm, straight mouth. His eyes were somewhat deeply set in his head, however, and there was a snake-like flattening at the upper part of his forehead, which detracted from his appearance. I almost involuntarily when I saw the head, pointed to it, and exclaimed—

"There is your prototype in your family, Miss Northcott."

"Do you think so?" she said. "I am afraid you are paying me a very bad compliment. Uncle Anthony was always considered the black sheep of the family."

"Indeed," I answered; "my remark was an unfortunate one, then."

"Oh, don't mind that," she said; "I always thought myself that he was worth all of them put together. He was an officer in the Forty-first Regiment, and he was killed in action during the Persian War—so he died nobly, at any-rate."

"That's the sort of death I should like to die," said Cowles, his dark eyes flashing, as they would when he was excited; "I often wish I had taken to my father's profession instead of this vile pill-compounding drudgery."

"Come, Jack, you are not going to die any sort of death yet," she said, tenderly taking his hand in hers.

I could not understand the woman. There was such an extraordinary mixture of masculine decision and womanly tenderness about her, with the consciousness of something all her own in the background, that she fairly puzzled me. I hardly knew, therefore, how to answer Cowles when, as we walked down the street together, he asked the comprehensive question—

"Well, what do you think of her?"

"I think she is wonderfully beautiful," I answered guardedly.

"That, of course," he replied irritably. "You knew that before you came!"

"I think she is very clever too," I remarked.

Barrington Cowles walked on for some time, and then he suddenly turned on me with the strange question—

"Do you think she is cruel? Do you think she is the sort of girl who would take a pleasure in inflicting pain?"

"Well, really," I answered, "I have hardly had time to form an opinion."

We then walked on for some time in silence.

"She is an old fool," at length muttered Cowles. "She is mad."

"Who is?" I asked.

"Why, that old woman—that aunt of Kate's—Mrs. Merton, or whatever her name is."

Then I knew that my poor colourless friend had been speaking to Cowles, but he never said anything more as to the nature of her communication.

My companion went to bed early that night, and I sat up a long time by the fire, thinking over all that I had seen and heard. I felt that there was some mystery about the girl—some dark fatality so strange as to defy conjecture. I thought of Prescott's interview with her before their marriage, and the fatal termination of it. I coupled it with poor drunken Reeves' plaintive cry, "Why did she not tell me sooner?" and with the other words he had spoken. Then my mind ran over Mrs. Merton's warning to me, Cowles'

130

reference to her, and even the episode of the whip and the cringing dog.

The whole effect of my recollections was unpleasant to a degree, and yet there was no tangible charge which I could bring against the woman. It would be worse than useless to attempt to warn my friend until I had definitely made up my mind what I was to warn him against. He would treat any charge against her with scorn. What could I do? How could I get at some tangible conclusion as to her character and antecedents? No one in Edinburgh knew them except as recent acquaintances. She was an orphan, and as far as I knew she had never disclosed where her former home had been. Suddenly an idea struck me. Among my father's friends there was a Colonel Joyce, who had served a long time in India upon the staff, and who would be likely to know most of the officers who had been out there since the Mutiny. I sat down at once, and, having trimmed the lamp, proceeded to write a letter to the Colonel. I told him that I was very curious to gain some particulars about a certain Captain Northcott, who had served in the Forty-first Foot, and who had fallen in the Persian War. I described the man as well as I could from my recollection of the daguerreotype, and then, having directed the letter, posted it that very night, after which, feeling that I had done all that could be done, I retired to bed, with a mind too anxious to allow me to sleep.

PART II.

I got an answer from Leicester, where the Colonel resided, within two days. I have it before me as I write, and copy it verbatim.

"DEAR BOB," it said, "I remember the man well. I was with him at Calcutta, and afterwards at Hyderabad. He was a curious, solitary sort of mortal; but a gallant soldier enough, for he distinguished himself at Sobraon, and was wounded, if I remember right. He was not popular in his corps—they said he was a pitiless, cold-blooded fellow, with no geniality in him. There was a rumor, too, that he was a devil-worshipper, or something of that sort, and also that he had the evil eye, which, of course, was all nonsense. He had some strange theories, I remember, about the power of the human will and the effects of mind upon matter.

"How are you getting on with your medical studies? Never forget, my boy, that your father's son has every claim upon me, and that if I can serve you in any way I am always at your command.—Ever affectionately yours,

EDWARD JOYCE.

"*P.S.*—By the way, Northcott did not fall in action. He was killed after peace was declared in a crazy attempt to get some of the eternal fire from the sun-worshippers' temple. There was considerable mystery about his death."

I read this epistle over several times—at first with a feeling of satisfaction, and then with one of disappointment. I had come on some curious information, and yet hardly what I wanted. He was an eccentric man, a devil-worshipper, and rumoured to have the power of the evil eye. I could believe the young lady's eyes, when endowed with that cold, grey shimmer which I had noticed in them once or twice, to be capable of any evil which human eye ever wrought; but still the superstition was an effete one. Was there not more meaning in that sentence which followed—"He had theories of the power of the human will and of the effect of mind upon matter"? I remember having once read a quaint treatise, which I had imagined to be mere charlatanism at the time, of the power of certain human minds, and of effects produced by them at a distance. Was Miss Northcott endowed with some exceptional power of the sort? The idea grew upon me, and very shortly I had evidence which convinced me of the truth of the supposition.

It happened that at the very time when my mind was

132

dwelling upon this subject, I saw a notice in the paper that our town was to be visited by Dr. Messinger, the well-known medium and mesmerist. Messinger was a man whose performance, such as it was, had been again and again pronounced to be genuine by competent judges. He was far above trickery, and had the reputation of being the soundest living authority upon the strange pseudo-sciences of animal magnetism and electro-biology. Determined, therefore, to see what the human will could do, even against all the disadvantages of glaring footlights and a public platform, I took a ticket for the first night of the performance, and went with several student friends.

We had secured one of the side boxes, and did not arrive until after the performance had begun. I had hardly taken my seat before I recognised Barrington Cowles, with his *fiancée* and old Mrs. Merton, sitting in the third or fourth row of the stalls. They caught sight of me at almost the same moment, and we bowed to each other. The first portion of the lecture was somewhat commonplace, the lecturer giving tricks of pure legerdemain, with one or two manifestations of mesmerism, performed upon a subject whom he had brought with him. He gave us an exhibition of clairvoyance too, throwing his subject into a trance, and then demanding particulars as to the movements of absent friends, and the whereabouts of hidden objects all of which appeared to be answered satisfactorily. I had seen all this before, however. What I wanted to see now was the effect of the lecturer's will when exerted upon some independent member of the audience.

He came round to that as the concluding exhibition in his performance. "I have shown you," he said, "that a mesmerized subject is entirely dominated by the will of the mesmerizer. He loses all power of volition, and his very thoughts are such as are suggested to him by the master-mind. The same end may be attained without any preliminary process. A strong will can, simply by virtue of its strength, take possession of a weaker one, even at a distance, and can regulate the impulses and the actions of the owner of it. If there was one man in the world who had

133

a very much more highly-developed will than any of the rest of the human family, there is no reason why he should not be able to rule over them all, and to reduce his fellow-creatures to the condition of automatons. Happily there is such a dead level of mental power, or rather of mental weakness, among us that such a catastrophe is not likely to occur; but still within our small compass there are variations which produce surprising effects. I shall now single out one of the audience, and endeavour 'by the mere power of will' to compel him to come upon the platform, and do and say what I wish. Let me assure you that there is no collusion, and that the subject whom I may select is at perfect liberty to resent to the uttermost any impulse which I may communicate to him."

With these words the lecturer came to the front of the platform, and glanced over the first few rows of the stalls. No doubt Cowles' dark skin and bright eyes marked him out as a man of a highly nervous temperament for the mesmerist picked him out in a moment, and fixed his eyes upon him. I saw my friend give a start of surprise, and then settle down in his chair, as if to express his determination not to yield to the influence of the operator. Messinger was not a man whose head denoted any great brain-power, but his gaze was singularly intense and penetrating. Under the influence of it Cowles made one or two spasmodic motions of his hands, as if to grasp the sides of his seat, and then half rose, but only to sink down again, though with an evident effort. I was watching the scene with intense interest, when I happened to catch a glimpse of Miss Northcott's face. She was sitting with her eyes fixed intently upon the mesmerist, and with such an expression of concentrated power upon her features as I have never seen on any other human countenance. Her jaw was firmly set, her lips compressed, and her face as hard as if it were a beautiful sculpture cut out of the whitest marble. Her eyebrows were drawn down, however, and from beneath them her grey eyes seemed to sparkle and gleam with a cold light.

I looked at Cowles again, expecting every moment to see him rise and obey the mesmerist's wishes, when there came from the platform a short, gasping cry as of a man utterly worn out and prostrated by a prolonged struggle. Messinger was leaning against the table, his hand to his forehead, and the perspiration pouring down his face. "I won't go on," he cried, addressing the audience. "There is a stronger will than mine acting against me. You must excuse me for to-night." The man was evidently ill, and utterly unable to proceed, so the curtain was lowered, and the audience dispersed, with many comments upon the lecturer's sudden indisposition.

I waited outside the hall until my friend and the ladies came out. Cowles was laughing over his recent experience.

"He didn't succeed with me, Bob," he cried triumphantly, as he shook my hand. "I think he caught a Tartar that time."

"Yes," said Miss Northcott, "I think that Jack ought to be very proud of his strength of mind; don't you, Mr. Armitage?"

"It took me all my time, though," my friend said seriously. "You can't conceive what a strange feeling I had once or twice. All the strength seemed to have gone out of me—especially just before he collapsed himself."

I walked round with Cowles in order to see the ladies home. He walked in front with Mrs. Merton, and I found myself behind with the young lady. For a minute or so I walked beside her without making any remark, and then I suddenly blurted out, in a manner which must have seemed somewhat brusque to her—

"You did that, Miss Northcott."

"Did what?" she asked sharply.

"Why, mesmerized the mesmerizer—I suppose that is the best way of describing the transaction."

"What a strange idea!" she said, laughing. "You give me credit for a strong will then?"

"Yes," I said. "For a dangerously strong one."

"Why dangerous?" she asked, in a tone of surprise.

"I think," I answered, "that any will which can exercise such power is dangerous—for there is always a chance of its being turned to bad uses."

"You would make me out a very dreadful individual,

135

Mr. Armitage," she said; and then looking up suddenly in my face—"You have never liked me. You are suspicious of me and distrust me, though I have never given you cause."

The accusation was so sudden and so true that I was unable to find any reply to it. She paused for a moment, and then said in a voice which was hard and cold—

"Don't let your prejudice lead you to interfere with me however, or say anything to your friend, Mr. Cowles, which might lead to a difference between us. You would find that to be very bad policy."

There was something in the way she spoke which gave an indescribable air of a threat to these few words.

"I have no power," I said, "to interfere with your plans for the future. I cannot help, however, from what I have seen and heard, having fears for my friend."

"Fears!" she repeated scornfully. "Pray, what have you seen and heard. Something from Mr. Reeves, perhaps—I believe he is another of your friends?"

"He never mentioned your name to me," I answered, truthfully enough. "You will be sorry to hear that he is dying." As I said it we passed by a lighted window, and I glanced down to see what effect my words had upon her. She was laughing—there was no doubt of it; she was laughing quietly to herself. I could see merriment in every feature of her face. I feared and mistrusted the woman from that moment more than ever.

We said little more that night. When we parted she gave me a quick, warning glance, as if to remind me of what she had said about the danger of interference. Her cautions could have made little difference to me could I have seen my way to benefiting Barrington Cowles by anything which I might say. But what could I say? I might say that her former suitors had been unfortunate. I might say that I believed her to be a cruel-hearted woman. I might say that I considered her to possess wonderful, and almost preter-natural powers. What impression would any of these ac-cusations make upon an ardent lover—a man with my friend's enthusiastic temperament? I felt that it would be useless to advance them, so I was silent.

And now I come to the beginning of the end. Hitherto much has been surmise and inference and hearsay. It is my painful task to relate now, as dispassionately and as accurately as I can, what actually occurred under my own notice, and to reduce to writing the events which preceded the death of my friend.

Towards the end of the winter Cowles remarked to me that he intended to marry Miss Northcott as soon as possible—probably some time in the spring. He was, as I have already remarked, fairly well off, and the young lady had some money of her own, so that there was no pecuniary reason for a long engagement. "We are going to take a little house out at Corstorphine," he said. "and we hope to see your face at our table, Bob, as often as you can possibly come." I thanked him, and tried to shake off my apprehensions, and persuade myself that all would yet be well.

It was about three weeks before the time fixed for the marriage, that Cowles remarked to me one evening that he feared he would be late that night. "I have had a note from Kate," he said, "asking me to call about eleven o'clock tonight, which seems rather a late hour, but perhaps she wants to talk over something quietly after old Mrs. Merton retires."

It was not until after my friend's departure that I suddenly recollected the mysterious interview which I had been told of as preceding the suicide of young Prescott. Then I thought of the ravings of poor Reeves, rendered more tragic by the fact that I had heard that very day of his death. What was the meaning of it all? Had this woman some baleful secret to disclose which must be known before her marriage? Was it some reason which forbade her to marry? Or was it some reason which forbade others to marry her? I felt so uneasy that I would have followed Cowles, even at the risk of offending him, and endeavoured to dissuade him from keeping his appointment, but a glance at the clock showed me that I was too late.

I was determined to wait up for his return, so I piled some coals upon the fire and took down a novel from the shelf. My thoughts proved more interesting than the book, however, and I threw it on one side. An indefinable feeling of anxiety and depression weighed upon me. Twelve o'clock came, and then half-past, without any sign of my friend. It was nearly one when I heard a step in the street outside, and then a knocking at the door. I was surprised, as I knew that my friend always carried a key—however, I hurried down and undid the latch. As the door flew open I knew in a moment that my worst apprehensions had been fulfilled. Barrington Cowles was leaning against the railings outside with his face sunk upon his breast, and his whole attitude expressive of the most intense despondency. As he passed in he gave a stagger, and would have fallen had I not thrown my left arm around him. Supporting him with this, and holding the lamp in my other hand, I led him slowly upstairs into our sitting-room. He sank down upon the sofa without a word. Now that I could get a good view of him, I was horrified to see the change which had come over him. His face was deadly pale, and his very lips were bloodless. His cheeks and forehead were clammy, his eyes glazed, and his whole expression altered. He looked like a man who had gone through some terrible ordeal, and was thoroughly unnerved.

"My dear fellow, what is the matter?" I asked, breaking the silence. "Nothing amiss, I trust? Are you unwell?"

"Brandy!" he gasped. "Give me some brandy!"

I took out the decanter, and was about to help him, when he snatched it from me with a trembling hand, and poured out nearly half a tumbler of the spirit. He was usually a most abstemious man, but he took this off at a gulp without adding any water to it. It seemed to do him good, for the color began to come back to his face, and he leaned upon his elbow.

"My engagement is off, Bob," he said, trying to speak calmly, but with a tremor in his voice which he could not conceal. "It is all over."

"Cheer up!" I answered, trying to encourage him. "Don't get down on your luck. How was it? What was it all about?"

"About?" he groaned, covering his face with his hands. "If I did tell you, Bob, you would not believe it. It is too dreadful—too horrible—unutterably awful and incredible! O Kate, Kate!" and he rocked himself to and fro in his grief; "I pictured you an angel and I find you a——"

"A what?" I asked, for he had paused.

He looked at me with a vacant stare, and then suddenly burst out, waving his arms: "A fiend!" he cried. "A ghoul from the pit! A vampire soul behind a lovely face! Now, God forgive me!" he went on in a lower tone, turning his face to the wall; "I have said more than I should. I have loved her too much to speak of her as she is. I love her too much now."

He lay still for some time, and I had hoped that the brandy had had the effect of sending him to sleep, when he suddenly turned his face towards me.

"Did you ever read of were-wolves?" he asked.

I answered that I had.

"There is a story," he said thoughtfully, "in one of Marryat's books, about a beautiful woman who took the form of a wolf at night and devoured her own children. I wonder what put that idea into Marryat's head?"

He pondered for some minutes, and then he cried out for some more brandy. There was a small bottle of laudanum upon the table, and I managed, by insisting upon helping him myself, to mix about half a dram with the spirits. He drank it off, and sank his head once more upon the pillow. "Anything better than that," he groaned. "Death is better than that. Crime and cruelty; cruelty and crime. Anything is better than that," and so on, with the monotonous refrain, until at last the words became indistinct, his eyelids closed over his weary eyes, and he sank into a profound slumber. I carried him into his bedroom without arousing him; and making a couch for myself out of the chairs, I remained by his side all night.

In the morning Barrington Cowles was in a high fever. For weeks he lingered between life and death. The highest medical skill of Edinburgh was called in, and his vigorous constitution slowly got the better of his disease. I nursed him during this anxious time; but through all his wild delirium and ravings he never let a word escape him which explained the mystery connected with Miss Northcott. Sometimes he spoke of her in the tenderest words and most loving voice. At others he screamed out that she was a fiend, and stretched out his arms, as if to keep her off. Several times he cried that he would not sell his soul for a beautiful face, and then he would moan in a most piteous voice, "But I love her—I love her for all that; I shall never cease to love her."

When he came to himself he was an altered man. His severe illness had emaciated him greatly, but his dark eyes had lost none of their brightness. They shone out with startling brilliancy from under his dark, overhanging brows. His manner was eccentric and variable —sometimes irritable, sometimes recklessly mirthful, but never natural. He would glance about him in a strange, suspicious manner, like one who feared something, and yet hardly knew what it was he dreaded. He never mentioned Miss Northcott's name—never until that fatal evening of which I have now to speak.

In an endeavour to break the current of his thoughts by frequent change of scene, I travelled with him through the highlands of Scotland, and afterwards down the east coast. In one of these peregrinations of ours we visited the Isle of May, an island near the mouth of the Firth of Forth, which, except in the tourist season, is singularly barren and desolate. Beyond the keeper of the lighthouse there are only one or two families of poor fisherfolk, who sustain a precarious existence by their nets, and by the capture of cormorants and solan geese. This grim spot seemed to have such a fascination for Cowles that we engaged a room in one of the fishermen's huts, with the intention of passing a week or two there. I found it very dull, but the loneliness appeared to be a relief to my friend's mind. He lost the look of apprehension which had become habitual to him, and became something like his old self. He would wander round the island all day, looking down from the summit of the great cliffs which gird it round, and watching the long green waves as they came booming in and burst in a shower of spray over the rocks beneath.

One night—I think it was our third or fourth on the island—Barrington Cowles and I went outside the cottage before retiring to rest, to enjoy a little fresh air, for our room was small, and the rough lamp caused an unpleasant odour. How well I remember every little circumstance in connection with that night! It promised to be tempestuous, for the clouds were piling up in the north-west, and the dark wrack was drifting across the face of the moon, throwing alternate belts of light and shade upon the rugged surface of the island and the restless sea beyond.

We were standing talking close by the door of the cottage, and I was thinking to myself that my friend was more cheerful than he had been since his illness, when he gave a sudden, sharp cry, and looking round at him I saw, by the light of the moon, an expression of unutterable horror come over his features. His eyes became fixed and staring, as if riveted upon some approaching object, and he extended his long thin forefinger, which quivered as he pointed.

"Look there!" he cried. "It is she! It is she! You see her there coming down the side of the brae." He gripped me convulsively by the wrist as he spoke. "There she is, coming towards us!"

"Who?" I cried, straining my eyes into the darkness.

"She—Kate—Kate Northcott!" he screamed. "She has come for me. Hold me fast, old friend. Don't let me go!"

"Hold up, old man," I said, clapping him on the shoulder. "Pull yourself together; you are dreaming; there is nothing to fear."

"She is gone!" he cried, with a gasp of relief. "No, by heaven! there she is again, and nearer—coming nearer. She told me she would come for me, and she keeps her word."

"Come into the house," I said. His hand, as I grasped it, was as cold as ice.

"Ah, I knew it!" he shouted. "There she is, waving her arms. She is beckoning to me. It is the signal. I must go. I am coming, Kate; I am coming!"

I threw my arms around him, but he burst from me with

superhuman strength, and dashed into the darkness of the night. I followed him, calling to him to stop, but he ran the more swiftly. When the moon shone out between the clouds I could catch a glimpse of his dark figure, running rapidly in a straight line, as if to reach some definite goal. It may have been imagination, but it seemed to me that in the flickering light I could distinguish a vague something in front of him—a shimmering form which eluded his grasp and led him onwards. I saw his outlines stand out hard against the sky behind him as he surmounted the brow of a little hill, then he disappeared, and that was the last ever seen by mortal eye of Barrington Cowles.

The fishermen and I walked round the island all that night with lanterns, and examined every nook and corner without seeing a trace of my poor lost friend. The direction in which he had been running terminated in a rugged line of jagged cliffs overhanging the sea. At one place here the edge was somewhat crumbled, and there appeared marks upon the turf which might have been left by human feet. We lay upon our faces at this spot, and peered with our lanterns over the edge, looking down on the boiling surge two hundred feet below. As we lay there, suddenly, above the beating of the waves and the howling of the wind, there rose a strange wild screech from the abyss below. The fishermen—a naturally superstitious race —averred that it was the sound of a woman's laughter, and I could hardly persuade them to continue the search. For my own part I think it may have been the cry of some sea-fowl startled from its nest by the flash of the lantern. However that may be, I never wish to hear such a sound again.

And now I have come to the end of the painful duty which I have undertaken. I have told as plainly and as accurately as I could the story of the death of John Barrington Cowles, and the train of events which preceded it. I am aware that to others the sad episode seemed commonplace enough. Here is the prosaic account which appeared in the *Scotsman* a couple of days afterwards:—

"Sad Occurrence on the Isle of May.—The Isle of May has been the scene of a sad disaster. Mr. John Barrington Cowles, a gentleman well known in University circles as a most distinguished student, and the present holder of the Neil Arnott prize for physics, has been recruiting his health in this quiet retreat. The night before last he suddenly left his friend, Mr. Robert Armitage, and he has not since been heard of. It is almost certain that he has met his death by falling over the cliffs which surround the island. Mr. Cowles' health has been failing for some time, partly from over-study and partly from worry connected with family affairs. By his death the University loses one of her most promising alumni."

I have nothing more to add to my statement. I have unburdened my mind of all that I know. I can well conceive that many, after weighing all that I have said, will see no ground for an accusation against Miss Northcott. They will say that, because a man of a naturally excitable disposition says and does wild things, and even eventually commits self-murder after a sudden and heavy disappointment, there is no reason why vague charges should be advanced against a young lady. To this, I answer that they are welcome to their opinion. For my own part, I ascribe the death of William Prescott, of Archibald Reeves, and of John Barrington Cowles to this woman with as much confidence as if I had seen her drive a dagger into their hearts.

You ask me, no doubt, what my own theory is which will explain all these strange facts. I have none, or, at best, a dim and vague one. That Miss Northcott possessed extraordinary powers over the minds, and through the minds over the bodies, of others, I am convinced, as well as that her instincts were to use this power for base and cruel purposes. That some even more fiendish and terrible phase of character lay behind this—some horrible trait which it was necessary for her to reveal before marriage—is to be inferred from the experience of her three loves, while the dreadful nature of the mystery thus revealed can only be surmised from the fact that the very mention of it drove from her those who had loved her so passionately. Their subsequent fate was, in my opinion, the result of her vindictive remembrance of their desertion of her, and that they were forewarned of it at the time was shown by the words of both Reeves and Cowles. Above this, I can say nothing. I lay the facts soberly before the public as they came under my notice. I have never seen Miss Northcott since, nor do I wish to do so. If by the words I have written I can save any one human being from the snare of those bright eyes and that beautiful face, then I can lay down my pen with the assurance that my poor friend has not died altogether in vain.

THE DOOR OF UNREST

By O. Henry

O. Henry was one of America's and one of the world's greatest writers of the short story. Most famed for his mastery of the surprise ending, which he refined into superlative art, his work possessed the "realism" that Theodore Dreiser promoted as the passion of his life, in a form so sublime that it was transmuted into art.

In the realm of the supernatural, O. Henry is primarily renowned for a single masterpiece, "The Furnished Room." It not only happens to be a bonafide ghost story, it is also one of his finest works. An accounting of the number of times it has been anthologized would require a bibliographer of prodigious and tireless talent. The Young Man, searching hopelessly through the rooming houses of New York for a trace of the girl he loves, realizes his search has ended when the room he has rented is filled "with the strong, sweet odour of mignonette," the fragrance that was part of her. It clings to him for awhile, and then is lost. No interrogation of the landlady can produce a description of an occupant of the room remotely resembling his sought-for human treasure.

Yet, he needs no further message. He plugs up the cracks on the door and turns on the gas. Several floors below, the landlady drinking beer with her cleaning woman is congratulated on having withheld the fact that a

145

young girl committed suicide by gas only a week prior to the young man's coming.

In every book on the strange and the supernatural, "The Furnished Room" is listed as O. Henry's sole contribution to the literature of the bizarre and unusual. Overlooked is "The Door of Unrest," published in *Cosmopolitan* for April, 1904. It is a remarkable tale based on The Wandering Jew legend. In fact, there is a penetrating insistence that while the legend is true, the wanderer is not a Jew at all, but a Gentile. O. Henry's background knowledge of the legend is so extensive that he must have done deliberate research on the topic. The story is a masterpiece in which he alternately taunts and tantalizes his readers. Is the character in question the Wandering Jew in fact, or a drunken, conscience-stricken Irish shoemaker, with a vivid imagination and a penchant for exploring old books?

O. Henry straddles the fence, but his allegory is crystal clear. There are thousands, perhaps millions in the world, with the unbearable conscience of an act which doom them "to tarry until he comes."

THE DOOR OF UNREST

By O. Henry

I sat, an hour by sun, in the editor's room of the Montopolis "Weekly Bugle." I was the editor.

The saffron rays of the declining sunlight filtered through the cornstalks in Micajah Widdup's garden-patch, and cast an amber glory upon my paste-pot. I sat at the editorial desk in my non-rotary revolving chair, and prepared my editorial against the oligarchies. The room, with its one window, was already a prey to the twilight. One by one, with my trenchant sentences, I lopped off the heads of the political hydra, while I listened, full of kindly peace, to the home-coming cow-bells and wondered what Mrs. Flanagan was going to have for supper.

Then in from the dusky, quiet street there drifted and

perched himself upon a corner of my desk old Father Time's younger brother. His face was beardless and as gnarled as an English walnut. I never saw clothes such as he wore. They would have reduced Joseph's coat to a monochrome. But the colors were not the dyer's. Stains and patches and the work of sun and rust were responsible for the diversity. On his coarse shoes was the dust, conceivably, of a thousand leagues. I can describe him no further except to say that he was little and weird and old, old—I began to estimate in centuries when I saw him. Yes; and I remember that there was an odor, a faint odor like aloes, or possibly like myrrh or leather; and I thought of museums.

And then I reached for a pad and pencil, for business is business, and visits of the oldest inhabitants are sacred and honorable, requiring to be chronicled.

"I am glad to see you, sir," I said. "I would offer you a chair, but—you see, sir," I went on, "I have lived in Montopolis only three weeks, and I have not met many of our citizens." I turned a doubtful eye upon his dust-stained shoes, and concluded with a newspaper phrase, "I suppose that you reside in our midst?"

My visitor fumbled in his raiment, drew forth a soiled card and handed it to me. Upon it was written, in plain but unsteadily formed characters, the name "Michob Ader."

"I am glad you called, Mr. Ader," I said. "As one of our older citizens, you must view with pride the recent growth and enterprise of Montopolis. Among other improvements, I think I can promise that the town will now be provided with a live, enterprising newspa——"

"Do ye know the name on that card?" asked my caller, interrupting me.

"It is not a familiar one to me," I said.

Again he visited the depths of his ancient vestments. This time he brought out a torn leaf of some book of journal, brown and flimsy with age. The heading of the page was "The Turkish Spy," in old-style type; the printing upon it was this:

"There is a man come to Paris in this year 1643 who pretends to have lived these sixteen hundred years. He

147

says of himself that he was a shoemaker in Jerusalem at the time of the Crucifixion; that his name is Michob Ader; and that when Jesus, the Christian Messias, was condemned by Pontius Pilate, the Roman president, he paused to rest while bearing his cross to the place of crucifixion before the door of Michob Ader. The shoemaker struck Jesus with his fist, saying: 'Go; why tarriest thou?' The Messias answered him: 'I indeed am going; but thou shalt tarry until I come'; therebye condemning him to live until the day of judgment. He lives forever, but at the end of every hundred years he falls into a fit or trance, on recovering from which he finds himself in the same state of youth in which he was when Jesus suffered, being then about thirty years of age.

"Such is the story of the Wandering Jew, as told by Michob Ader, who relates—" Here the printing ended.

I must have muttered aloud something to myself about the Wandering Jew, for the old man spake up, bitterly and loudly.

" 'Tis a lie," said he, "like nine-tenths of what ye call history. 'Tis a Gentile I am, and no Jew. I am after footing it out of Jerusalem, my son; but if that makes me a Jew, then everything that comes out of a bottle is babies' milk. Ye have my name on the card ye hold; and ye have read the bit of paper they call 'The Turkish Spy' that printed the news when I stepped into their office on the 12th day of June in the year 1643, just as I have called upon ye today."

I laid down my pencil and pad. Clearly it would not do. Here was an item for the local column of the "Bugle" that—but it would not do. Still, fragments of the impossible "personal" began to flit through my conventionalized brain. "Uncle Michob is as spry on his legs as a young chap of only a thousand or so." "Our venerable caller relates with pride that George Wash—no, Ptolemy the Great—once dandled him on his knee at his father's house." "Uncle Michob says that our wet spring was nothing in comparison with the dampness that ruined the crops around Mount Ararat when he was a boy——" But no, no—it would not do.

148

I was trying to think of some conversational subject with which to interest my visitor, and was hesitating between walking-matches and the Pliocene age, when the old man suddenly began to weep poignantly and distressfully.

"Cheer up, Mr. Ader," I said, a little awkwardly; "this matter may blow over in a few hundred years more. There has already been a decided reaction in favor of Judas Iscariot and Colonel Burr and the celebrated violinist, Signor Nero. This is the age of whitewash. You must not allow yourself to become downhearted."

Unknowingly, I had struck a chord. The old man blinked belligerently through his senile tears.

" 'Tis time," he said, "that the liars be doin' justice to somebody. Yer historians are no more than a pack of old women gabblin' at a wake. A finer man than the Imperor Nero niver wore sandals. Man, I was at the burnin' of Rome. I knowed the imperor well, for in thim days I was a well-known char-racter. In thim days they had rayspect for a man that lived forever.

"But 'twas of the Imperor Nero I was goin' to tell ye. I struck into Rome, up the Appian Way, on the night of July the 16th, the year 64. I had just stepped down by way of Siberia and Afghanistan; and one foot of me had a frostbite, and the other a blister burned by the sand of the desert; and I was feelin' a bit blue from doin' patrol duty from the north pole down to the Last Chance corner in Patagonia, and bein' miscalled a Jew in the bargain. Well, I'm tellin' ye I was passin' the Circus Maximus, and it was dark as pitch over that way, and then I heard somebody sing out, 'Is that you, Michob?'

"Over ag'inst the wall, hid out amongst a pile of barrels and old dry-goods boxes, was the Imperor Nero wid his togy wrapped around his toes, smokin' a long, black segar.

" 'Have one, Michob?' says he.

" 'None of the weed for me,' says I—'naytlier pipe nor segar. What's the use,' says I, 'of smokin' when ye've not got the ghost of a chance of killin' yeself by doin' it?'

" 'True for ye, Michob Ader, my perpetual Jew,' says the imperor; 'ye're not always wandering. Sure, 'tis danger
149

gives the spice to our pleasures—next to their bein' forbidden.'

" 'And for what,' says I, 'do ye smoke be night in dark places widout even a cinturion in plain clothes to attend ye?'

" 'Have ye ever heard, Michob,' says the imperor, 'of predestinarianism?'

" 'I've had the cousin of it,' says I. 'I've been on the trot with pedestrianism for many a year, and more to come, as ye well know.'

" 'The longer word,' says me friend Nero, 'is the tachin' of this new sect of people they call the Christians. 'Tis them that's raysponsible for me smokin' be night in holes and corners of the dark.'

"And then I sets down and takes off a shoe and rubs me foot that is frosted, and the imperor tells me about it. It seems that since I passed that way before, the imperor had mandamused the impress wid a divorce suit, and Missis Poppaea, a cilibrated lady, was ingaged, widout riferences, as housekeeper at the palace. 'All in one day,' says the imperor, 'she puts up new lace windy-curtains in the palace and joins the anti-tobacco society, and whin I feels the need of a smoke I must be after sneakin' out to these piles of lumber in the dark.' So there in the dark me and the imperor sat, and I told him of me travels. And when they say the imperor was an incindiary, they lie. 'Twas that night the fire started that burnt the city. 'Tis my opinion that it began from a stump of segar that he threw down among the boxes. And 'tis a lie that he fiddled. He did all he could for six days to stop it, sir."

And now I tetected a new flavor to Mr. Michob Ader. It had not been myrrh or balm or hyssop that I had smelled. The emanation was the odor of bad whisky—and, worse still, of low comedy—the sort that small humorists manufacture by clothing the grave and reverend things of legend and history in the vulgar, topical frippery that passes for a certain kind of wit. Michob Ader was an impostor, claiming nineteen hundred years, and playing his part with the decency of respectable lunacy, I could endure; but as a tedious wag, cheapening his
150

egregious story with song-book levity, his importance as an entertainer grew less.

And then, as if he suspected my thoughts, he suddenly shifted his key.

"You'll excuse me, sir," he whined, "but sometimes I get a little mixed in my head. I am a very old man; and it is hard to remember everything."

I knew that he was right, and that I should not try to reconcile him with Roman history; so I asked for news concerning other ancients with whom he had walked familiar.

Above my desk hung an engraving of Raphael's cherubs. You could yet make out their forms, though the dusk blurred their outlines strangely.

"Ye calls them 'cher-rubs,'" cackled the old man. "Babes, ye fancy they are, with wings. And there's one wid legs and a bow and arrow that ye call Cupid—I know where they was found. The great-great-great-grandfather of thim all was a billy-goat. Bein' an editor, sir, do ye happen to know where Solomon's Temple stood?"

I fancied that it was in—in—Persia? Well, I did not know.

" 'Tis not in history nor in the Bible where it was. But I saw it, myself. The first pictures of cher-rubs and cupids was sculptured upon thim walls and pillars. Two of the biggest, sir, stood in the adytum to form the baldachin over the Ark. But the wings of thim sculptures was intindid for horns. And the faces was the faces of goats. Ten thousand goats there was in and about the temple. And your cher-rubs was billy-goats in the days of King Solomon, but the painters misconstrued the horns into wings.

"And I knew Tamerlane, the lame Timur, sir, very well. I saw him at Keghut and at Zaranj. He was a little man, no larger than yeself, with hair the color of an amber pipe-stem. They buried him at Samarkand. I was at the wake, sir. Oh, he was a fine-built man in his coffin, six feet long, with black whiskers to his face. And I see 'em throw turnips at the Imperor Vispacian, in Africa. All over the world I have tramped, sir, without the body of me findin' any rest. 'Twas so commanded. I saw Jerusalem destroyed, and Pompeii go up in the fireworks; and I was at the coronation of Charlemagne and the lynchin' of Joan of Arc. And everywhere I go there comes storms and revolutions and plagues and fires. 'Twas so commanded. Ye have heard of the Wandering Jew. 'Tis all so, except that divil a bit am I a Jew. But history lies, as I have told ye. Are ye quite sure, sir, that ye haven't a drop of whisky convenient? Ye well know that I have many miles of walkin' before me."

"I have none," said I, "and, if you please, I am about to leave for my supper."

I pushed my chair back creakingly. This ancient landlubber was becoming as great an affliction as any crossbowed mariner. He shook a musty effluvium from his piebald clothes, overturned my inkstand and went on with his insufferable nonsense.

"I wouldn't mind it so much," he complained, "if it wasn't for the work I must do on Good Fridays. Ye know about Pontius Pilate, sir, of course. His body, whin he killed himself, was pitched into a lake on the Alps mountains. Now, listen to the job that 'tis mine to perform on the night of ivery Good Friday. The ould divil goes down in the pool and drags up Pontius, and the water is bilin' and spewin' like a wash-pot. And the ould divil sets the body on top of a throne on the rocks; and thin comes me share of the job. Oh, sir, ye would pity me thin—ye would pray for the poor Wandering Jew that niver was a Jew if ye could see the horror of the thing that I must do. 'Tis I that must fetch a bowl of water and kneel down before it till it washes its hands. I declare to ye that Pontius Pilate, a man dead two thousand years, dragged up with the lake slime coverin' him and fishes wrigglin' inside of him widout eyes, and in the discomposition of the body, sits there, sir, and washes his hands in the bowl I hold for him on Good Fridays. 'Twas so commanded."

Clearly, the matter had progressed far beyond the scope of the "Bugle's" local column. There might have been employment here for the alienist or for those who circulate the pledge; but I had had enough of it. I got up, and repeated that I must go.

At this he seized my coat, groveled upon my desk and burst again into distressful weeping. Whatever it was about, I said to myself that his grief was genuine.

"Come, now, Mr. Ader," I said, soothingly; "what is the matter?"

The answer came brokenly through his racking sobs: "Because I would not . . . let the poor Christ . . . rest . . . upon my step."

His hallucination seemed beyond all reasonable answer; yet the effect of it upon him scarcely merited disrespect. But I knew nothing that might assuage it; and I told him once more that both of us should be leaving the office at once.

Obedient at last, he raised himself from my disheveled desk, and permitted me to half lift him to the floor. The gale of his grief had blown away his words; his freshet of tears had soaked away the crust of his grief. Reminiscence died in him—at least, the coherent part of it.

" 'Twas me that did it," he muttered, as I led him toward the door—"me, the shoemaker of Jerusalem."

I got him to the sidewalk, and in the augmented light I saw that his face was seared and lined and warped by a sadness almost incredibly the product of a single lifetime.

And then high up in the firmamental darkness we heard the clamant cries of some great, passing birds. My Wandering Jew lifted his hand, with side-tilted head.

"The Seven Whistlers!" he said, as one introduces well-known friends.

"Wild geese," said I; "but I confess that their number is beyond me."

"They follow me everywhere," he said. " 'Twas so commanded. What ye heard is the souls of the seven Jews that helped with the Crucifixion. Sometimes they're plovers, and sometimes geese, but ye'll find them always flyin' where I go."

I stood, uncertain how to take my leave. I looked down the street, shuffled my feet, looked back again—and felt my hair rise. The old man had disappeared.

And then my capillaries relaxed, for I dimly saw him footing it away through the darkness. But he walked so swiftly and silently, and contrary to the gait promised by his age, that my composure was not all restored, though I knew not why.

That night I was foolish enough to take down some dust-covered volumes from my modest shelves. I searched "Hermippus Redivivus" and "Salathiel" and the "Pepys Collection" in vain. And then in a book called "The Citizen of the World," and in one two centuries old, I came upon what I desired. Michob Ader had indeed come to Paris in the year 1643, and related to "The Turkish Spy" an extraordinary story. He claimed to be the Wandering Jew, and that——

But here I fell asleep, for my editorial duties had not been light that day.

Judge Hoover was the "Bugle's" candidate for congress. Having to confer with him, I sought his home early the next morning; and we walked together down-town through a little street with which I was infamiliar.

"Did you ever hear of Michob Ader?" I asked him, smiling.

"Why, yes," said the judge. "And that reminds me of my shoes he has for mending. Here is his shop now."

Judge Hoover stepped into a dingy, small shop. I looked up at the sign, and saw "Mike O'Bader, Boot and Shoe Maker," on it. Some wild geese passed above, honking clearly. I scratched my ear and frowned, and then trailed into the shop.

There sat my Wandering Jew on his shoemaker's bench, trimming a half-sole. He was drabbled with dew, grass-stained, unkempt and miserable; and on his face was still the unexplained wretchedness, the problematic sorrow, the esoteric woe that had been written there by nothing less, it seemed, than the stylus of the centuries.

Judge Hoover inquired kindly concerning his shoes. The old shoemaker looked up, and spoke sanely enough. He had been ill, he said, for a few days. The next day the shoes would be ready. He looked at me, and I could see that I had no place in his memory. So out we went, and on our way.

"Old Mike," remarked the candidate, "has been on one of his sprees. He gets crazy-drunk regularly once a month. But he's a good shoemaker."

"What is his history?" I inquired.

"Whisky," epitomized Judge Hoover. "That explains him."

I was silent, but I did not accept the explanation. And so, when I had the chance, I asked old man Sellers, who browsed daily on my exchanges.

"Mike O'Bader," said he, "was makin' shoes in Montopolis when I come here goin' on fifteen year ago. I guess whisky's his trouble. Once a month he gets off the track, and stays so a week. He's got a rigmarole somethin' about his bein' a Jew pedler that he tells ev'rybody. Nobody won't listen to him any more. When he's sober he ain't sich a fool—he's got a sight of books in the back room of his shop that he reads. I guess you can lay all his trouble to whisky."

But again I would not. Not yet was my Wandering Jew rightly construed for me. I trust that women may not be allowed a title to all the curiosity in the world. So when Montopolis' oldest inhabitant (some ninety score years younger than Michob Ader) dropped in to acquire promulgation in print, I siphoned his perpetual trickle of reminiscence in the direction of the uninterpreted maker of shoes.

Uncle Abner was the Complete History of Monotopolis, bound in butternut.

"O'Bader," he quavered, "come here in '69. He was the first shoemaker in the place. Folks generally considers him crazy at times now. But he don't harm nobody. I s'pose drinkin' upsot his mind—yes, drinkin' very likely done it. It's a powerful bad thing, drinkin'. I'm an old, old man, sir, and I never yet see no good in drinkin'."

I felt disappointment. I was willing to admit drink in the case of my shoemaker, but I preferred it as a recourse instead of a cause. Why had he pitched upon his perpetual, strange note of the Wandering Jew? Why his unutterable grief during his aberration? I could not yet accept whisky—as an explanation.

"Did Mike O'Bader ever have a great loss or trouble of any kind?" I asked.

"Lemme see! About thirty year ago there was somethin' of the kind, I recollect. Montopolis, sir, in them days used to be a mighty strict place.

"Well, Mike O'Bader had a daughter then—a right pretty girl. She was too gay a sort for Montopolis; so one day she slips off to another town and runs away with a circus. It was two years before she comes back, all fixed up in fine clothes and rings and jewelry, to see Mike. He wouldn't have nothin' to do with her, so she stays around town awhile, anyway. I reckon the menfolks wouldn't have raised no objections, but the women egged 'em on to order her to leave town. But she had plenty of spunk, and told 'em to mind their own business.

"So, one night they decided to run her away. A crowd of men and women drove her out of her house, and chased her with sticks and stones. She run to her father's door, callin' for help. Mike opens it, and when he sees who it is he hits her with his fist and knocks her down and shuts the door.

"And then the crowd kept on chunkin' her till she run clear out of town. And then next day they finds her drowned dead in Hunter's millpond. I mind it all now. That was thirty year ago."

I leaned back in my non-rotary revolving chair, and nodded gently, like a mandarin, at my paste-pot.

"When old Mike has a spell," went on Uncle Abner, tepidly garrulous, "he thinks he's the Wanderin' Jew."

"He is," said I, nodding away.

And Uncle Abner cackled insinuatingly at the editor's remark, for he was expecting at least a "stickful" in the "Personal Notes" of the "Bugle."

THURLOW'S GHOST STORY

By John Kendrick Bangs

At the turn of the century, John Kendrick Bangs was un-questionably one of America's foremost humorists. For a decade his books had seen edition after edition, and there were at least forty under his own name, but he was so fond of pen names that his true output may never be known. There was one peculiarity about Bangs' humor: it usually had to involve a ghost. To write at least nineteen books of humor about ghosts requires a preoccupation with the subject which is unusual, to say the least. Yet Bangs has never been regarded as a ghost-story writer and his name is rarely seen in books or articles on the supernatural. To make the matter all the more confusing, critics were quick to admit that Bangs' humor usually did not have a "message." When he called from their eternal sleep the shades of many of the greats of history, from Diogenes to George Washington, (in *A Houseboat On The Styx*, 1895), and brought them for an encore by popular de-mand in "The Pursuit of the Houseboat" (1897), his main purpose appeared to be banter and that was just what the readers wanted.

Judging by the success of his books, Bangs could have made a full-time living as a writer, but actually it was only a very vigorous avocation with him. He was usually the editor of some newspaper or magazine. His friends say that he was a spontaneous wit and far funnier in person than in his books. He was editorial writer on the world's first tabloid newspaper, *The Daily Continent,* which Frank A. Munsey began to publish on February 1, 1891. *The Daily Continent* only lasted four months, and was more distinguished for its fiction than its news, but Bangs had no trouble getting other connections. He had spent four years with *Life* (1884 to 1888) when it was a magazine of humor and satire. He shifted to *Harper's Monthly* from 1888 to 1899 and then was made editor of *Harper's Weekly,* until 1904, when he became editor of *Puck.* Through all of this the books kept flowing. And he also wrote an endless stream of verse under innumberable pen names. His poem "Honesty" appeared under the pen name of Carlyle Smith in the November 27, 1917 issue of *The Argosy*; and "The Age of the Camera" (originally titled "The Age of the Lens") appeared under the name Wilberforce Jenkins in *The Argosy*, of September 28, 1918.

It was Dorothy Scarborough, in her volume *The Supernatural in Modern English Fiction* (1918) who realized that some of Bangs' shorter ghost stories were valid contributions to the art and commented upon "Thurlow's Christmas Story," which is printed here as "Thurlow's Ghost Story." Even before Charles Dickens' *A Christmas Carol,* it had been the custom of leading magazines and newspapers to carry a ghost story for their December or Christmas edition. This tradition has not completey died out, even today. But in John Kendrick Bangs' time it was in full sway, and this is a remarkably effective presentation especially since Bangs was under commission to turn the story in by a deadline. It is superbly done, with a sublime note of irony, particularly for writers.

THURLOW'S GHOST STORY

By John Kendrick Bangs

I

(Being the Statement of Henry Thurlow, Author, to George Currier, Editor of the "Idler," a Weekly Journal of Human Interest.)

I have always maintained, my dear Currier, that if a man wishes to be considered sane, and has any particular regard for his reputation as a truth-teller, he would better keep silent as to the singular experiences that enter into his life. I have had many such experiences myself; but I have rarely confided them in detail, or otherwise, to those about me, because I know that even the most trustful of my friends would regard them merely as the outcome of an imagination unrestrained by conscience, or of a gradually weakening mind subject to hallucinations. I know them to be true, but until Mr. Edison or some other modern wizard has invented a search-light strong enough to lay bare the secrets of the mind and conscience of man, I cannot prove to others that they are not pure fabrications, or at least the conjurings of a diseased fancy. For instance, no man would believe me if I were to state to him the plain and indisputable fact that one night last month, on my way up to bed shortly after midnight, having been neither smoking nor drinking, I saw confronting me upon the stairs, with the moonlight streaming through the windows back of me, lighting up its face, a figure in which I recognized my very self in every form and feature. I might describe the chill of terror that struck to the very marrow of my bones, and wellnigh forced me to stagger backward down the stairs, as I noticed in the face of this confronting figure every indication of all the bad qualities which I know myself to possess, of every evil instinct which by no easy effort I have repressed heretofore, and realized that the *thing* was, as far as I knew, entirely independent of my true self, in which I hope at least the moral has made an

159

honest fight against the immoral always. I might describe this chill, I say, as vividly as I felt it at that moment, but it would be of no use to do so, because, however realistic it might prove as a bit of description, no man would believe that the incident really happened; and yet it did happen as truly as I write, and it has happened a dozen times since, and I am certain that it will happen a dozen times again, though I would give all that I possess to be assured that never again should that disquieting creation of mind or matter, whichever it may be, cross my path. The experience has made me afraid almost to be alone, and I have found myself unconsciously and uneasily glancing at my face in mirrors, in the plate-glass of show-windows on the shopping streets of the city, fearful lest I should find some of those evil traits which I have struggled to keep under so far, cropping out there where all the world, all *my* world, can see and wonder at, having known me always as a man of right doing and right feeling. Many a time in the night the thought has come to me with prostrating force, what if that thing were to be seen and recognized by others, myself and yet not my whole self, my unworthy self unrestrained and yet recognizable as Henry Thurlow.

I have also kept silent as to that strange condition of affairs which has tortured me in my sleep for the past year and a half; no one but myself has until this writing known that for that period of time I have a continuous, logical dream-life; a life so vivid and so dreadfully real to me that I have found myself at times wondering which of the two lives I was living and which I was dreaming; a life in which that other wicked self has dominated, and forced me to a career of shame and horror; a life which being taken up every time I sleep where it ceased with the awakening from a previous sleep, has made me fear to close my eyes in forgetfulness when others are near at hand, lest, sleeping, I shall let fall some speech that, striking on their ears, shall lead them to believe that in secret there is some wicked mystery connected with my life. It would be of no use for me to tell these things. It would merely serve to make my family and my friends uneasy about me if they were told in their awful detail, and so I have kept silent about them. To you alone, and now for the first time, have I hinted as to the troubles which have oppressed me for many days, and to you they are confided only because of the demand you have made that I explain to you the extraordinary complication in which the Christmas story sent you last week has involved me. You know that I am a man of dignity; that I am not a school-boy and a lover of childish tricks; and knowing that, your friendship, at least, should have restrained your tongue and pen when, through the former, on Wednesday, you accused me of perpetrating a trifling, and to you excessively embarrassing, practical joke—a charge which, at the moment, I was too overcome to refute; and through the latter, on Thursday, you reiterated the accusation, coupled with a demand for an explanation of my conduct satisfactory to yourself, or my immediate resignation from the staff of the *Idler*. To explain is difficult, for I am certain that you will find the explanation too improbable for credence, but explain I must. The alternative, that of resigning from your staff, affects not only my own welfare, but that of my children, who must be provided for; and if my post with you is taken from me, then are all resources gone. I have not the courage to face dismissal, for I have not sufficient confidence in my powers to please elsewhere to make me easy in my mind, or, if I could please elsewhere, the certainty of finding the immediate employment of my talents which is necessary to me, in view of the at present overcrowded condition of the literary field.

To explain, then, my seeming jest at your expense, hopeless as it appears to be, is my task; and to do so as completely as I can, let me go back to the very beginning.

In August you informed me that you would expect me to provide, as I have heretofore been in the habit of doing, a story for the Christmas issue of the *Idler;* that a certain position in the make-up was reserved for me, and that you had already taken steps to advertise the fact that the story would appear. I undertook the commission, and upon seven different occasions set about putting the narrative into shape. I found great difficulty, however, in doing so. For some reason or other I could not concentrate my mind upon the work. No sooner would I start in on one story than a better one, in my estimation, would suggest itself to me; and all the labor expended on the story already begun would be cast aside, and the new story set in motion. Ideas were plenty enough, but to put them properly upon paper seemed beyond my powers. One story, however, I did finish; but after it had come back to me from my typewriter I read it, and was filled with consternation to discover that it was nothing more nor less than a mass of jumbled sentences, conveying no idea to the mind—a story which had seemed to me in the writing to be incoherence—formless, without ideas—a bit of raving. It was then that I went to you and told you, as you remember, that I was worn out, and needed a month of absolute rest, which you granted. I left my work wholly, and went into the wilderness, where I could be entirely free from everything suggesting labor, and where no summons back to town could reach me. I fished and hunted. I slept; and although, as I have already said, in my sleep I found myself leading a life that was not only not to my taste, but horrible to me in many particulars, I was able to at the end of my vacation to come back to town greatly refreshed, and, as far as my feeling went, ready to undertake any amount of work. For two or three days after my return I was busy with other things. On the fourth day after my arrival you came to me, and said that the story must be finished at the very latest by October 15th, and I assured you that you should have it by that time. That night I set about it. I mapped it out, incident by incident, and before starting up to bed had actually written some twelve or fifteen hundred words of the opening chapter—it was to be told in four chapters. When I had gone thus far I experienced a slight return of one of my nervous chills, and, on consulting my watch, discovered that it was after midnight, which was a sufficient explanation of my nervousness: I was merely tired. I arranged my manuscripts on my table so that I might easily take up the work the following

162

morning. I locked up the windows and doors, turned out the lights, and proceeded up-stairs to my room.

It was then that I first came face to face with myself—that other self, in which I recognized, developed to the full, every bit of my capacity for an evil life.

Conceive of the situation if you can. Imagine the horror of it, and then ask yourself if it was likely that when next morning came I could by any possibility bring myself to my work-table in fit condition to prepare for you anything at all worthy of publication in the *Idler.* I tried. I implore you to believe that I did not hold lightly the responsibilities of the commission you had intrusted to my hands. You must know that if any of your writers has a full appreciation of the difficulties which are strewn along the path of an editor, I, who have myself had an editorial experience, have it, and so would not, in the nature of things, do anything to add to your troubles. You cannot but believe that I have made an honest effort to fulfil my promise to you. But it was useless, and for a week after that visitation was it useless for me to attempt the work. At the end of the week I felt better, and again I started in, and the story developed satisfactorily until—*it* came again. That figure which was my own figure, that face which was the evil counterpart of my own countenance, again rose up before me, and once more was I plunged into hopelessness.

Thus matters went on until the 14th day of October, when I received your peremptory message that the story must be forthcoming the following day. Needless to tell you that it was not forthcoming; but what I must tell you, since you do not know it, is that on the evening of the 15th day of October a strange thing happened to me, and in the narration of that incident, which I almost despair of your believing, lies my explanation of the discovery of October 16th, which has placed my position with you in peril.

At half-past seven o'clock on the evening of October 15th I was sitting in my library trying to write. I was alone. My wife and children had gone away on a visit to Massachusetts for a week. I had just finished my cigar, and had taken my pen in hand, when my front-door bell rang. Our maid, who is usually prompt in answering summonses of this nature, apparently did not hear the bell, for she did not respond to its clanging. Again the bell rang, and still did it remain unanswered, until finally, at the third ringing, I went to the door myself. On opening it I saw standing before me a man of, I should say, fifty odd years of age, tall, slender, pale-faced, and clad in sombre black. He was entirely unknown to me. I had never seen him before, but he had about him such an air of pleasantness and wholesomeness that I instinctively felt glad to see him, without knowing why or whence he had come.

"Does Mr. Thurlow live here?" he asked.

You must excuse me for going into what may seem to you to be petty details, but by a perfectly circumstantial account of all that happened that evening alone can I hope to give a semblance of truth to my story, and that it must be truthful I realize as painfully as you do.

"I am Mr. Thurlow," I replied.

"Henry Thurlow, the author?" he said, with a surprised look upon his face.

"Yes," said I; and then, impelled by the strange appearance of surprise on the man's countenance, I added, "don't I look like an author?"

He laughed, and candidly admitted that I was not the kind of looking man he had expected to find from reading my books, and then he entered the house in response to my invitation that he do so. I ushered him into my library, and, after asking him to be seated, inquired as to his business with me.

His answer was gratifying at least. He replied that he had been a reader of my writings for a number of years, and that for some time past he had had a great desire, not to say curiosity, to meet me and tell me how much he had enjoyed certain of my stories.

"I'm a great devourer of books, Mr. Thurlow," he said, "and I have taken the keenest delight in reading your verses and humorous sketches. I may go further, and say to you that you have helped me over many a hard place in

164

my life by your work. At times when I have felt myself worn out with my business, or face to face with some knotty problem in my career, I have found much relief in picking up and reading your books at random. They have helped me to forget my weariness or my knotty problems for the time being; and to-day, finding myself in this town, I resolved to call upon you this evening and thank you for all that you have done for me."

Thereupon we become involved in a general discussion of literary men and their works, and I found that my visitor certainly did have a pretty thorough knowledge of what has been produced by the writers of to-day. I was quite won over to him by his simplicity, as well as attracted to him by his kindly opinion of my own efforts, and I did my best to entertain him, showing him a few of my little literary treasures in the way of autograph letters, photographs, and presentation copies of well-known books from the authors themselves. From this we drifted naturally and easily into a talk on the methods; and when I had in a measure outlined to him the manner of life which I had adopted, telling him of my days at home, how little detail office-work I had, he seemed much interested with the picture—indeed, I painted the picture of my daily-routine in almost too perfect colors, for, when I had finished, he observed quietly that I appeared to him to lead the ideal life, and added that he supposed I knew very little unhappiness.

The remark recalled to me the dreadful reality, that through some perversity of fate I was doomed to visitations of an uncanny order which were practically destroying my usefulness in my profession and my sole financial resource.

"Well," I replied, as my mind reverted to the unpleasant predicament in which I found myself, "I can't say that I know little unhappiness. As a matter of fact, I know a great deal of that undesirable thing. At the present moment I am very much embarrassed through my absolute inability to fulfil a contract into which I have entered, and which should have been filled this morning. I was due to-

165

day with a Christmas story. The presses are waiting for it, and I am utterly unable to write it."

He appeared deeply concerned at the confession. I had hoped, indeed, that he might be sufficiently concerned to take his departure, that I might make one more effort to write the promised story. His solicitude, however, showed itself in another way. Instead of leaving me, he ventured the hope that he might aid me.

"What kind of a story is it to be?" he asked.

"Oh, the usual ghostly tale," I said, "with a dash of the Christmas flavor thrown in here and there to make it suitable to the season."

"Ah," he observed. "And you find your vein worked out?"

It was a direct and perhaps an impertinent question; but I thought it best to answer it, and to answer it as well without giving him any clew as to the real facts. I could not very well take an entire stranger into my confidence, and describe to him the extraordinary encounters I was having with an uncanny other self. He would not have believed the truth, hence I told him an untruth, and assented to his proposition.

"Yes," I replied, "the vein is worked out. I have written ghost stories for years now, serious and comic, and I am to-day at the end of my tether—compelled to move forward and yet held back."

"That accounts for it," he said, simply. "When I first saw you to-night at the door I could not believe that the author who had provided me with so much merriment could be so pale and worn and seemingly mirthless. Pardon me, Mr. Thurlow, for my lack of consideration when I told you that you did not appear as I had expected to find you."

I smiled my forgiveness, and he continued:

"It may be," he said, with a show of hesitation—"it may be that I have come not altogether inopportunely. Perhaps I can help you."

I smiled again. "I should be most grateful if you could," I said.

166

"But you doubt my ability to do so?" he put in. "Oh—well—yes—of course you do; and why shouldn't you? Nevertheless, I have noticed this: At times when I have been baffled in my work a mere hint from another, from one who knew nothing of my work, has carried me on to a solution of my problem. I have read most of your writings, and I have thought over some of them many a time, and I have even had ideas for stories, which, in my own conceit, I have imagined were good enough for you, and I have wished that I possessed your facility with the pen that I might make of them myself what I thought you would make of them had they been ideas of your own."

The old gentleman's pallid face reddened as he said this, and while I was hopeless as to anything of value resulting from his ideas, I could not resist the temptation to hear what he had to say further, his manner was so deliciously simple, and his desire to aid me so manifest. He rattled on with suggestions for a half-hour. Some of them were good, but none were new. Some were irresistibly funny, and did me good because they made me laugh, and I hadn't laughed naturally for a period so long that it made me shudder to think of it, fearing lest I should forget how to be mirthful. Finally I grew tired of his persistence, and, with a very ill-concealed impatience, told him plainly that I could do nothing with his suggestions, thanking him, however, for the spirit of kindliness which had prompted him to offer them. He appeared somewhat hurt, but immediately desisted, and when nine o'clock came he rose up to go. As he walked to the door he seemed to be undergoing some mental struggle, to which, with a sudden resolve, he finally succumbed, for, after having picked up his hat and stick and donned his overcoat, he turned to me and said:

"Mr. Thurlow, I don't want to offend you. On the contrary, it is my dearest wish to assist you. You have helped me, as I have told you. Why may I not help you?"

"I assure you, sir—" I began, when he interrupted me.

"One moment, please," he said, putting his hand into the inside pocket of his black coat and extracting from it an envelope addressed to me. "Let me finish: it is the

167

whim of one who has an affection for you. For ten years I have secretly been at work myself on a story. It is a short one, but it has seemed good to me. I had a double object in seeking you out to-night. I wanted not only to see you, but to read my story to you. No one knows that I have written it; I had intended it as a surprise to my—to my friends. I had hoped to have it published somewhere, and I had come here to seek your advice in the matter. It is a story which I have written and rewritten and rewritten time and time again in my leisure moments during the ten years past, as I have told you. It is not likely that I shall ever write another. I am proud of having done it, but I should be prouder yet if it—if it could in some way help you. I leave it with you, sir, to print or to destroy; and if you print it, to see it in type will be enough for me; to see your name signed to it will be a matter of pride to me. No one will ever be the wiser, for, as I say, no one knows I have written it, and I promise you that no one shall know of it if you decide to do as I not only suggest but ask you to do. No one would believe me after it has appeared as *yours,* even if I should forget my promise and claim it as my own. Take it. It is yours. You are entitled to it as a slight measure of repayment for the debt of gratitude I owe you."

He pressed the manuscript into my hands, and before I could reply had opened the door and disappeared into the darkness of the street. I rushed to the sidewalk and shouted out to him to return, but I might as well have saved my breath and spared the neighborhood, for there was no answer. Holding his story in my hand, I re-entered the house and walked back into my library, where, sitting and reflecting upon the curious interview, I realized for the first time that I was in entire ignorance as to my visitor's name and address.

I opened the envelope hoping to find them, but they were not there. The envelope contained merely a finely written manuscript of thirty odd pages unsigned.

And then I read the story. When I began it was with a half-smile upon my lips, and with a feeling that I was wasting my time. The smile soon faded, however; after reading the first paragraph there was no question of wasted time. The story was a masterpiece. It is needless to say to you that I am not a man of enthusiasms. It is difficult to arouse that emotion in my breast, but upon this occasion I yielded to a force too great for me to resist. I have read the tales of Hoffmann and of Poe, the wondrous romances of De La Motte Fouque, the unfortunately little-known tales of the lamented Fitz-James O'Brien, the weird tales of writers of all tongues have been thoroughly sifted by me in the course of my reading, and I say to you now that in the whole of my life I never read one story, one paragraph, one line, that could approach in vivid delineation, in weirdness of conception, in anything, in any quality which goes to make up the truly great story, that story which came into my hands as I have told you. I read it once and was amazed. I read it a second time and was—tempted. It was mine. The writer himself had authorized me to treat it as if it were my own; had voluntarily sacrificed his own claim to its authorship that he might relieve me of my very pressing embarrassment. Not only this; he had almost intimated that in putting my name to his work I should be doing him a favor. Why not do so, then, I asked myself; and immediately my better self rejected the idea as impossible. How could I put out as my own another man's work and retain my self-respect? I resolved on another and better course—to send you the story in lieu of my own with a full statement of the circumstances under which it had come into my possession, when that demon rose up out of the floor at my side, this time more evil of aspect than before, more commanding in its manner. With a groan I shrank back into the cushions of my chair, and by passing my hands over my eyes tried to obliterate forever the offending sight; but it was useless. The uncanny thing approached me, and as truly as I write sat upon the edge of my couch, where for the first time it addressed me.

"Fool!" it said, "how can you hesitate? Here is your position: you have made a contract which must be filled; you are already behind, and in a hopeless mental state.

Even granting that between this and to-morrow morning you could put together the necessary number of words to fill the space allotted to you, what kind of a thing do you think that story would make? It would be a mere raving like that other precious effort of August. The public, if by some odd chance it ever reached them, would think your mind was utterly gone; your reputation would go with that verdict. On the other hand, if you do not have the story ready by to-morrow, your hold in the *Idler* will be destroyed. They have their announcements printed, and your name and portrait appear among those of the prominent contributors. Do you suppose the editor and publisher will look leniently upon your failure?"

"Considering my past record, yes," I replied. "I have never yet broken a promise to them."

"Which is precisely the reason why they will be severe with you. You, who have been regarded as one of the few men who can do almost any kind of literary work at will—you, of whom it is said that your 'brains are on tap'—will they be lenient with *you*? Bah! Can't you see that the very fact of your invariable readiness heretofore is going to make your present unreadiness a thing incomprehensible?"

"Then what shall I do?" I asked. "If I can't, I can't, that is all."

"You can. There is the story in your hands. Think what it will do for you. It is one of the immortal stories—"

"You have read it, then?" I asked.

"Haven't you?"

"Yes—but—"

"It is the same," it said with a leer and a contemptuous shrug. "You and I are inseparable. Aren't you glad?" it added, with a laugh that grated on every fibre of my being. I was too overwhelmed to reply, and it resumed: "It is one of the immortal stories. We agree to that. Published over your name, your name will live. The stuff you write yourself will give you present glory; but when you have been dead ten years people won't remember your name even—unless I get control of you, and in that case there is

170

a very pretty though hardly a literary record in store for you."

Again it laughed harshly, and I buried my face in the pillows of my couch, hoping to find relief there from this dreadful vision.

"Curious," it said. "What you call your decent self doesn't dare look me in the eye! What a mistake people make who say that the man who won't look you in the eye is not to be trusted! As if mere brazenness were a sign of honesty; really, the theory of decency is the most amusing thing in the world. But come, time is growing short. Take that story. The writer gave it to you. Begged you to use it as your own. It is yours. It will make your reputation, and save you with your publishers. How can you hesitate?"

"I shall not use it!" I cried, desperately.

"You must—consider your children. Suppose you lose your connection with these publishers of yours?"

"But it would be a crime."

"Not a bit of it. Whom do you rob? A man who voluntarily came to you, and gave you that of which you rob him. Think of it as it is—and act, only act quickly. It is now midnight."

The tempter rose up and walked to the other end of the room, whence, while he pretended to be looking over a few of my books and pictures, I was aware he was eying me closely, and gradually compelling me by sheer force of will to do a thing which I abhorred. And I—I struggled weakly against the temptation, but gradually, little by little, I yielded, and finally succumbed altogether. Springing to my feet, I rushed to the table, seized my pen, and signed my name to the story.

"There!" I said. "It is done. I have saved my position and made my reputation, and am now a thief!"

"As well as a fool," said the other, calmly. "You don't mean to say you are going to send that manuscript in as it is?"

"Good Lord!" I cried. "What under heaven have you been trying to make me do for the last half hour?"

"Act like a sane being," said the demon. "If you send

that manuscript to Currier he'll know in a minute it isn't yours. He knows you haven't an amanuensis, and that handwriting isn't yours. Copy it."

"True!" I answered. "I haven't much of a mind for details to-night. I will do as you say."

I did so. I got out my pad and pen and ink, and for three hours diligently applied myself to the task of copying the story. When it was finished I went over it carefully, made a few minor corrections, signed it, put it in an envelope, addressed it to you, stamped it, and went out to the mailbox on the corner, where I dropped it into the slot, and returned home. When I had returned to my library my visitor was still there.

"Well," it said, "I wish you'd hurry and complete this affair. I am tired, and wish to go."

"You can't go too soon to please me," said I, gathering up the original manuscripts of the story and preparing to put them away in my desk.

"Probably not," it sneered. "I'll be glad to go too, but I can't go until that manuscript is destroyed. As long as it exists there is evidence of your having appropriated the work of another. Why, can't you see that? Burn it."

"I can't see my way clear in crime!" I retorted. "It is not in my line."

Nevertheless, realizing the value of his advice, I thrust the pages one by one into the blazing log fire, and watched them as they flared and flamed and grew to ashes. As the last page disappeared in the embers the demon vanished. I was alone, and throwing myself down for a moment's reflection upon my couch, was soon lost in sleep.

It was noon when I again opened my eyes, and, ten minutes after I awakened, your telegraphic summons reached me.

"Come down at once," was what you said, and I went; and then came the terrible *dénouement,* and yet a *dénouement* which was pleasing to me since it relieved my conscience. You handed me the envelope containing the story.

"Did you send that?" was your question.

172

"I did—last night, or rather early this morning. I mailed it about three o'clock," I replied.

"I demand an explanation of your conduct," said you.

"Of what?" I asked.

"Look at your so-called story and see. If this is a practical joke, Thurlow, it's a damned poor one."

I opened the envelope and took from it the sheets I had sent you—twenty-four of them.

They were every one of them as blank as when they left the paper-mill!

You know the rest. You know that I tried to speak; that my utterance failed me; and that, finding myself unable at the time to control my emotions, I turned and rushed madly from the office, leaving the mystery unexplained. You know that you wrote demanding a satisfactory explanation of the situation or my resignation from your staff.

This, Currier, is my explanation. It is all I have. It is absolute truth. I beg you to believe it, for if you do not, then is my condition a hopeless one. You will ask me perhaps for a *résumé* of the story which I thought I had sent you.

It is my crowning misfortune that upon that point my mind is an absolute blank. I cannot remember it in form or in substance. I have racked my brains for some recollection of some small portion of it to help to make my explanation more credible, but, alas! it will not come back to me. If I were dishonest I might fake up a story to suit the purpose, but I am not dishonest. I came near to doing an unworthy act; I did do an unworthy thing, but by some mysterious provision of fate my conscience is cleared of that.

Be sympathetic, Currier, or, if you cannot, be lenient with me this time. *Believe, believe, believe,* I implore you. Pray let me hear from you at once.

(Signed) HENRY THURLOW.

II

(Being a Note from George Currier, Editor of the "Idler," to Henry Thurlow, Author.)

Your explanation has come to hand. As an explanation it isn't worth the paper it is written on, but we are all agreed here that it is probably the best bit of fiction you ever wrote. It is accepted for the Christmas issue. Enclosed please find check for one hundred dollars.

Dawson suggests that you take another month up in the Adirondacks. You might put in your time writing up some account of that dream-life you are leading while you are there. It seems to me there are possibilities in the idea. The concern will pay all expenses. What do you say?

(Signed)   Yours ever,   G.C.

THE MAN WITH THE BROWN BEARD

By Nathaniel T. Babcock

Fame is conferred in strange ways. The first truly comprehensive listing of "Fantasy in the Munsey Periodicals" was compiled by William H. Evans, and serialization of it had begun in the Winter, 1946-47 issue of *Fantasy Comentator*. This was an event of major importance to every important collector of fantasy, since the Munsey magazines, collectively, comprising such publications as *The Argosy, The All-Story Magazine, The Cavalier, The Scrap Book* and various others, had published more stories of this type throughout the long years of their existence than any other non-specialized periodicals in the world.

The earliest fantasy story listed on any of William Evan's bibliographies was "The Man With the Brown Beard" by Nathaniel T. Babcock, which first appeared in the February, 1896 issue of *The Argosy*. As time has shown, this was not the case and there are a number of prior titles, but no revised index has ever been published and until this day Babcock's story bears the distinction of being number one in a truly monumental listing.

In 1939, The Frank A. Munsey Company began a reprint magazine of classics of fantasies from their back issues titled *Famous Fantastic Mysteries,* and it prospered well enough to spawn a companion *Fantastic Novels.* Many of the most famous stories mentioned by old-time readers were reprinted, but never "The Man With the Brown Beard".

To compound the situation, at the time that story was published, *The Argosy* had converted from a boy's publication to an adult magazine, with slick paper and illustrated articles in competition with such formidible publication's as the firm's own *Munsey's,* The *Cosmopolitan, McClure's, The Century, Harper's, The Atlantic Monthly* and numerous others, and its circulation approached nadir. Therefore, it was very difficult for even a specialist collector to find.

As the years progressed, possession of this story became an obsession with many collectors. They didn't care if it was good, bad or indifferent; they just wanted to find out what it was all about.

Nathaniel T. Babcock may conceivably have been a prominent author in his day, but time has drawn a curtain over his name. No reference to him can be found in the very exhaustive files to which this compiler has access. However, "The Man With the Brown Beard," though based on an old theme, the exchange of bodies, does happen to be an extraordinarily powerful tale of horror. It is anything but a filler, or a carelessly tossed off bit of hackwork. It is a story that holds one attention, displays considerable adroitness in plotting, and finishes with enough power to evoke a queasy feeling in the pit of the stomach.

Though I know the Munsey Index watchers would be satisfied just to read the story, it is a real satisfaction to me that the story is well worth reading.

THE MAN WITH THE BROWN BEARD

By Nathaniel T. Babcock

If my pen continues to remain a pen and my ink changes not into blood or wine until the purpose is accomplished, I shall, I think, succeed in giving to the public a tale as wondrous strange as any to which the world has, for many years, listened. There is nothing in the appearance of this gracefully pointed bit of steel and its cedar wood handle, as I hold it between my eyes and the lamplight, to suggest a possibility of its suddenly becoming a serpent's tail or a devil's divining rod, nor do I perceive in the contents of my crystal inkstand anything beyond a superior quality of black writing fluid; and yet for caution's sake, and lest I all unexpectedly become again the victim of a supernatural practical joke, I beg the privilege of prefacing my story with the above improbable, as you will say, provisos.

There are going to be in the unfolding of this narrative, as everybody will discover, several very embarrassing factors, chief of which is this, that although I suppose I am relating certain extraordinary events which have happened to me, I have no positive means of knowing that such is the case. The two of us, by whom I mean Harry Jessup (who certainly once was and still seems to be) and poor John Sutherland (who clearly now is not), are so closely, so intimately, connected—soul intertwined, if I may use the expression—that I (or is it he?) who speak can be certain of all things more easily than of my (or is it his?) identity.

Clearly, however, we shall not get on at all at this rate. Though honestly endeavoring to enlighten, I perceive I am but mystifying my readers. Let me quiet my nerves with one draught of this wholesome wine (here's to you, poor John Sutherland!) and proceed as calmly as I can with my story.

One year ago tonight I was lying in the Tombs prison, New York City, under sentence of death for murder. I was guiltless. This fact, unfortunately, was known only to myself. In justice to my memory (or should I say in justice to the memory of John Sutherland?) I must briefly relate the circumstances which led to that error of justice which condemned an innocent man to the gallows.

I was born (that is, supposing I am the person who, though contrary to all external appearances, I still believe myself to be) in the city of London, England. If I had parents I never knew them; neither was I acquainted with brothers, sisters, or relatives even of a remote degree. I purloined what little knowledge I had of the world from the tips of gentlemen at the backs of whose chairs I stood during the breakfast and dining hours at some of the most reputable eating houses in London. I got a bit of book learning at an evening school, and other odds and ends of accomplishments I picked up at merry places by gaslight. It was while employed at one of those "Homes of Harmony" that I obtained that knowledge of the pianoforte which, in spite of its superficiality, is today so great a source of wonder to those persons with whom I am now surrounded. I read more than fellows of my sort, and, as a consequence, soon became educated beyond my station and emigrated to America. Upon my arrival in New York I found work at fair wages in an eating house somewhere east of Broadway. I was put to share the room of an Italian waiter, a surly, ill favored person, who, within two months after I had taken quarters with him, cut his throat while I lay by his side, a circumstance which brought him no greater harm than it brought to me, since on the following morning I was thrown into jail, and six weeks later removed to the Tombs under sentence of death.

A year ago tonight, at just about this hour, to avoid the gaze of the curious newspaper writers who clustered thick about the stove at the end of the narrow corridor upon which my cell opened, and who (the jailer having permitted me the freedom of the passage) pitilessly noted down my every despairing movement, I stepped back behind my grated door and threw myself face downward upon my narrow bed. I remember that the cot was covered with a coarse gray blanket, across which, near either end, was woven a narrow strip of red. The jailer rattled the grating of my door and spoke kindly, advising me to remove my coat and boots and get a bit of sleep. I lifted my head as he spoke. The blood red streak in the blanket was immediately under my chin; I had thrown myself down, throat across it. I sat bolt upright on the bed. My hand went involuntarily to my throat. The jailer's kindly face seemed to my terror stricken vision the face of a devil. I knew that within a few hours I was to be murdered, and he was to be

178

my murderer. I felt that I ought to hate him; that if I were half a man I would seize his beard and batter his head upon the rusty iron of the cage. Yet, when I spoke, my voice was low, courteous, even modestly submissive, as I thanked him for his attention. Great God! think of it—I thanked the man who stood there at my cell door keeping watch over a stalled ox for the coming of the butcher.

He turned to go. The rage which in my soul had found birth and death without power of expression was followed by a frantic grief, an overwhelming self pity. I longed to throw myself upon my knees before the retreating figure and beg for mercy, but again my limbs refused to act, and as the jailer faced the grating for a last look at his victim, I think he must have seen a smile—who knows, perhaps a grin?—upon my face, for he brightened, and said, "That's right, Jessup; I'm glad to see you keeping up a good heart."

Tell me the face is the soul's mirror! The soul is as powerless to control the body as the body is powerless to control the soul. Rage, grief, despair, incite to action, and the body mocks them all. True, I am an unlearned and an unlettered man, but of the soul's relation to the body who on earth should know more than I have been taught?

It is possible that the suicide, just prior to the carrying out of his purpose, is made acquainted with that sickening, muscle relaxing, nerve tightening despair which comes to the man who is to be executed tomorrow, but I do not think so. In the case of suicide there must be (and this, before long, I shall fully discover) an absence of that pitiful helplessness which tears the heartstrings of the man who is to be put to death by his fellows. Oh, the grief of it! The haunting horror of any human form! With pistol in hand, even when its cold round muzzle is pressed against his throbbing temple; even to that fractional part of a second in which the cruel deed is done, the suicide is soothed by a consciousness of an optional escape. There is no time fixed. He is the master of his punishment. The inexorable is lacking in the refinement of his torture.

When the jailer had disappeared from view I sank back upon the cot. I turned myself upon my back and looked at the plain white ceiling. I tried to people this vague surface with heaven's lamps—to imagine it was God's firmament. There were the countless stars twinkling as merrily as though no sorrow anywhere existed. Spread out around me was the mighty ocean, foaming and rolling near by, then stretching off like a great, black, quiet plain. I was once more upon the steamer, the accursed steamer that brought me to New York to be killed. The motion, how delightful! swing so, swing so. My hands went to the side of the cot for the protection of my balance. Oh, this motion! now up, now down! The stars, how bright! The waves! see, see how high. Mercy! what pleasure. Great tears flow down my cheeks. Crash! we've struck! We're sinking! My fingers go to my eyes; rub, rub, and there is again the white ceiling. No stars? I spring to my feet. No ocean? A prison cell; death by strangulation in the morning.

I staggered to the cell door; I pressed my cheek against the grating and was able to see a portion of the group of watchers at the end of the corridor. Their heads were together; somebody was relating a story. A fat man had his profile to me. From time to time his hands went down upon his knees with a slap, and his sides shook. He was being amused by reminiscences of the trusty jailer. Amused? These men being amused, and I——

I could no longer endure the sight of my fellow men. Again I threw myself upon the bed. The red stripe on the blanket had lost its terror. I saw nothing, thought of nothing, but men; crowds of men in black, coming after me! Coming with a rope to strangle me. I, a man like themselves, with head and legs and arms like theirs. They would take me by the hands and we should touch one another; they would look in my face and I should look in theirs, and nowhere, nowhere, would I find anybody to help me, to save me! Shut up in a cage awaiting the approach of my own species, sons of women, like myself; relentlessly coming, to put me to death! Coming perhaps from happy firesides, and waiting only until I should be dead to return to their wives and little ones; not a man among them but would lend an arm to the meanest cripple on the street, yet coming, coming to butcher me. Could the good Lord, who made us all in a world of sin and suffering, approve it? I got down upon my knees; I tried to pray, but just as comfort seemed approaching, a sudden awful sensation, as of the presence of the executioner standing at my back, rope in hand, brought me trembling to my feet. Again I fell exhausted on my bed. And now a mighty terror of my own body seized upon me. My head was raised so that I saw the entire length of my figure. It seemed to me to be the body of a strangled corpse. I moved my foot to dispel the illusion, but with the cessation of its motion the frightful hallucination returned. I madly assisted the delusion. I crossed my hands on my breast; they seemed to become waxen, cold, and bloodless. I closed my eyes and pressed my elbows tightly against my sides to avoid contact with the linen of a coffin. A sickening nausea arose within me; my heart seemed turning over in its place, and then—consciousness ceased; merciful sleep had come to my relief.

*   *   *   *

I awoke with a start. When I make this statement I feel I am doing scant justice to an extraordinary phenomenon. How do I know that I ever awoke? May I not still be lying in a dream upon that prison bed? May not the gallows and rope be yet in store for me? Well, if such is the case, surely my supposing that it is not the case can do no harm. You, my mythical readers, will not worry over it if you are mythical, and if you are real, why, then I, too, must be real, and the phenomenon a reality. I think that I awoke suddenly, and with the thought of the dire business of the morning very present in my mind. It was broad daylight—the light of that day I had shivered to think of—the light which was to be a signal for all those men in black with crape on their arms to take their victim to the sacrifice. A film seemed stretched across the balls of my eyes, upon which were mirrored a multitude of colors that now, as my staring pupils dilated, took form in a hundred beautiful things. First of all, I seemed to see just in front of me the face of a pretty child smiling from out a halo of yellow hair; a sideway glance, and heavy curtains of some bright red material parted to permit my dazzled eyes to

181

behold a window flaming with reflections of the morning sunlight. Overhead my sky was a plane of brown and gold. My hand falling at my side rested upon a texture as soft as swansdown; my body undulated upon a bed softer than any it had ever before known.

It is now a year since the day of that awakening. I have been for the last ten minutes endeavoring to recall my first impressions, my earliest thoughts, as this scene, the beauty of which I have but hinted at, dawned upon my senses. I may have supposed myself in heaven, but, if so, the idea could have been no more than momentary, for it was impossible for one lying as I was lying, in a position commanding a view on all sides, not speedily to discover that he was the occupant of a very comfortable bed in a decidedly luxurious bedchamber. My little girl of the golden hair hung in a massive frame on the tinted wall directly opposite the foot of my bed; the window through which came in the early sunlight, was in a bow of the east wall; my brown and gold sky was excellent fresco, equal to anything I had ever seen in those establishments in which my livelihood had been gained on the other side of the water.

How long I had been staring at these marvelous surroundings I cannot say, when suddenly there came a soft rap at the door, which was on the right of the apartment, and a very cheery voice, the voice of a young girl, exclaimed, "Jacko! Jacko, are you going to sleep all day?"

I listened in amazement, and naturally made no reply.

"Jacko, I tell you," continued the pretty voice, "it's after eight o'clock, and we are all waiting for you."

Clearly the child was addressing some person whom she supposed to be in the room, of which I was the only occupant. The rapping on the door of an obviously impatient little fist continued. It was necessary to respond. I said "Hello!"

"All right," replied the little voice. "I'm glad you are awake at last; now do hurry."

Hurry? Hurry where? I had an engagement at seven o'clock. The child assured me, and a French clock on the mantel confirmed her statement, that it was past eight.

Where was I? What did it all mean? I softly protruded one foot from the yielding bedclothing and planted it upon the thick carpet on the floor. How warm and grateful was the sense! My other leg followed, and I stood erect. In what was I dressed! White linen, with beautiful scarlet loops in place of common buttonholes—the night robe of a prince! I smoothed the fabric with my hand, and was surprised to discover a roundness and plumpness in my limbs, of which I had never before been conscious. I put my hand to my bewildered head. A beard? A beard upon my face which had ever been beardless!

In the corner was a handsome dresser, surmounted by a high mirror. With wild, uncertain steps I crossed the room. The polished glass of the mirror showed the face of an utter stranger. Forgetful of the fact that, had he stood behind me, my own figure must have obscured his image, I wheeled about and confronted—no one. The room was occupied by myself alone. Again I faced the glass. There stood the stranger, with face as white as that of a corpse, and eyes that seemed starting from his head. I put my hand to my eyes; the specter in the glass imitated the motion. I screamed and fell to the floor, the image in the glass disappearing simultaneously with my fall. I had never fainted in my life, and I did not become unconscious. Lifting myself upon my elbow I looked around me.

The base of a wardrobe immediately opposite my point of vision was set with plate glass. In that mirror I again saw the stranger, lying, as I was lying, with his cheek upon the palm of his hand. I got upon my knees and clasped my hands. The figure in the glass followed each motion. I jumped to my feet. The head and shoulders of the image disappeared, but from the waist downward remained. I then perceived that the mirror in the base of the wardrobe was less than three feet high. It was, then, my own reflection that I saw! No, not my own reflection, for I was a man six feet in height, slimly built, with light hair and blue eyes, and a beardless face. The object in the glass was scarcely five feet nine, inclined to stoutness, with short, curly brown hair, and a heavy dark beard. I turned to the mirror above the dresser, my knees quaking under me from consternation. The ashen face of the brown bearded stranger again confronted me. I lifted my finger to my lips in a dazed, meaningless way, and the man in the glass did the same. Just then there came a loud knock at the door, and a hearty voice said,

"Open the door for a moment, Jack; I've something to say to you."

Was the voice addressing me? I stood like a stone alternately growing hot and cold.

"I say, old man, open the door," continued the voice from without.

Half unconsciously I approached the door and pushed back the bolt that held it. A handsome young fellow, rosy and radiant as from a brisk walk, and bearing a striking resemblance to the image in the glass, rushed in as the bolt was drawn, and clapping his hands upon my shoulders, exclaimed, "Jack, old man, it's all fixed; we're going with you. The governor gave in at the last when mother, Nell, and I all got after him in a bunch. But what's the matter with you, Jack?" (holding me at arm's length and peering anxiously into my face.) "You look as if you'd seen a ghost. Here, Nell! mother! Jack is fainting."

I have before mentioned that I never faint; neither did I then, though I doubt not Walter had good cause to imagine that I would. I felt the blood leaving my body; I became limp in the strong young fellow's arms as he tenderly assisted me to the sofa. Atrracted by his call there entered a moment later a matronly looking woman of fifty or thereabouts, followed by a girl of fifteen, whom I at once, recognized as the original of the portrait, grown a few summers older. Both threw themselves on their knees at my feet. Mother (I gave the title by which I today address that estimable lady) placed her arm lovingly around my shoulder, and drew my head toward her own, while Nell grasped one of my hands and began to kiss it gently.

"My poor boy," began the lady, "you have overtaxed yourself, just as I feared you would, and the anticipation of this morning's event, in the weakened condition of your nerves, has made you ill. I shall be glad when the ceremony is over and you are comfortably off."

Great heavens! What was the lady speaking of? "The anticipation of this morning's event"? "weakened my nerves"? "comfortably off"? What does it mean? Had I really been executed in the prison yard, and was I in some place of purgatory, waiting to go through the agony under different surroundings? Was this the beginning of a sinner's eternity? Were these people fiends in the guise of angels? Was I to go on forever, being executed in different shapes?

"Come, Jack dear," continued the good lady; "Walter will help you with your clothes, and after a good breakfast and a cup of hot coffee you'll be yourself again."

"And," chimed in the pretty little maiden, "we won't tell Julie what a devoted husband she is to have. A man—oh, Jacko, for shame!—who becomes ill on his wedding day merely at the thought of being married!"

During all this time my lips had refused to utter a sound, and I could now only exclaim, "Heaven have mercy on me!" a remark which caused Walter and his mother to hold a hurried conversation at the back of the sofa, and then to leave the room, saying cheerily that they would not be gone a moment.

Left alone with me, the young girl clapped her hands over my knees, and looking in my face, said, "Now, Jacko, my darling, tell me what is the matter? You won't keep anything from your own Nell? I admire Julie and I respect her, but if this marriage is going to make you unhappy, I'll break it off if I have to go to the girl myself and tell her that you do not love her. Oh, Jacko, my best, my dearest brother, tell me what is the matter?"

"Please leave me," was all that I could articulate.

"Dear Jacko," cried the affectionate girl, "I cannot leave you. You never spoke to me so before. My brother, my dear, dear brother!"

"Where is your brother?" I cried.

There was probably a look in my eyes that terrified the girl, for she arose to her feet, and with tears streaming from her eyes left the room.

I was alone, and again approached the glass. The brown bearded man looked haggard and unnatural. "For the love

185

of Him who made us," I cried, speaking to the stranger in the mirror, "tell me who you are and who am I?"

"Why, Jack, my boy, what is the matter?"

I felt a strong hand upon my shoulder, and, turning, confronted a pleasant mannered, middle age gentleman whom I rightly inferred to be a physician. Just behind stood Walter and his mother. I do not know whether it was the strong individuality of the doctor that impressed me with a sense of the reality of my surroundings, which up to this moment had seemed illusory and vague, but I suddenly felt a warmth of blood returning to my limbs and a sense of rest and security in my condition; a determination to drift whithersoever fate might lead me. A smile must have shown itself in my face, for the doctor turned to the anxious lady and said, "It is nothing, my dear madam; mere nervous excitement which will soon pass away." He then prepared a potion, which I cheerfully swallowed. Walter inquired whether he should not assist me to dress, and I assented. The drollery of my existence now began to take precedence of all other emotions. The brown bearded man in the glass was no longer an object of terror in my eyes; he became amusing. I saw, I could not fail to see, that his motions and actions were entirely in my control. Little by little, I came to a graceful acceptance of my new identity. A man who has been hanged, said I to myself, cannot be chooser in any subsequent allotment of events. If this is hell, I must admit it is an unexpectedly agreeable hell, and if it is heaven, I should certainly ask for nothing better.

This mild acceptance of my extraordinary fate, at that time, was probably due in a large measure to the drug which the doctor had administered—a powerful narcotic, no doubt—that quieted my nerves and caused my troubled brain to become languid. Piloted by Walter, who happily insisted upon keeping hold of my arm, I passed through a spacious and handsome hall and down a broad pair of stairs to a very luxurious breakfast room, where, for the first time, I met the head of the family, a mild eyed man past middle age, who, during the strange scenes of the morning, had been absent from the house, and who now greeted me very tenderly. Throughout the breakfast which followed, I remained completely silent. There was a large pier glass opposite me in which, with quiet amusement, I beheld the brown bearded man put morsels of food into his rather handsome mouth, I myself enjoying the sensation of swallowing the same. I did not fail to notice that my silence and evident preoccupation was a source of keen distress to the others at the table, but I was powerless to improve matters.

As the soothing effects of the doctor's potion wore away my thoughts became more troublesome and bewildering, until finally, unable to remain any longer quiet, I arose from the table and fled to an adjoining room. There seemed to have been an intention on the part of some member of the family to follow me, but the head of the house exclaimed, "No, let Jack alone; he'll come out all right presently."

Upon a table in the room in which I had taken refuge lay a newspaper. I picked it up. The date—that dreadful date to which for weeks I had looked forward with sickening consternation—showed me that it was the latest issue. The paper was called the *Denver Tribune,* and was printed in Denver, Colorado. As I scanned the sheet, a faint recollection as of something heard in childhood came upon me. I recalled a conversation caught in a fragmentary way years before, while standing at dinner behind two English noblemen. They were talking of this "Denver, Colorado." What were they saying? Oh, yes, they were speaking of Denver as the chief city of a cattle raising province in the United States.

I was then still in the United States! In Denver! But how in Denver? How anywhere except in a murderer's cell in the Tombs prison, New York?

While pondering with aching head upon these questions, my eyes encountered the following paragraph:

Harry Jessup, the brutal murderer of Eduardo Italiani, is to be hanged in the Tombs prison, New York City, at seven o'clock this morning.

Again and again I read this paragraph. My eyes devoured the three brief lines of print till every word a and letter seemed eating its way into my soul. "Harry Jessup, the brutal murderer of Eduardo Italiani, is to be hanged! Is to be hanged? A clock on the mantel struck nine. "Is to be hanged at the Tombs Prison, New York City, at seven o'clock this morning." Is to be hanged? I, Harry Jessup, am to be—my God! what does it mean? This is the day, this is the morning, and the sun, which rose at five o'clock, is four hours old! My eyes dropped again upon the paper which had fallen on my lap, and I read the following notice:

The marriage of Mr. John Sutherland (better known to his countless friends in Denver as "Jack" Sutherland) to Miss Julie Chamberlain, will take place at the residence of the bride this morning. It is to be a very quiet affair, only the immediate friends of the two families having received cards.

For a moment my brain seemed to be bursting. The sickening nausea which I felt in the prison had returned, and then, quietly, like a great awakening of some hitherto dormant intellectual faculties, there stole into my soul the consciousness of a miracle performed. I had not suffered at the hangman's hands. I lived. I had never ceased to live. Every action of my life was accessible to memory. I was still Harry Jessup. Were I dead, had I passed into another world, my store of knowledge would of necessity be increased or diminished; but it remained the same. I mentally ran over my past life, and at every station found proof of a personal and intimate knowledge of but one man, and that man was Harry Jessup. I arose and approached the glass. There stood the brown bearded stranger.

I looked in the face, and *knew that he had stolen my soul.* The mirror showed me the body of John Sutherland, with the soul of Harry Jessup. But the soul of the man whose body I wore, what of it?

The sound of voices, subdued but earnest, came to my

ears from the adjoining room. The name of "Jack," "dear Jack," was constantly upon the lips of the distressed parents of the loving brother and sister. It needed no marvelous perspicacity for me, stranger as I was to them all, to discover that this "brother Jack," into whose suit of flesh I had unwittingly stepped, was a very dearly beloved member of the household. I learned from such fragments of their talk as reached my ears, that the loved ones were sorely troubled at my (at John Sutherland's) behavior, and were at a loss what to do. The newspaper paragraph, taken in connection with the young lady's remark in the chamber, made it obvious to me that this was to have been the wedding day of the brown bearded man, and I readily understood the dilemma into which was (or rather my) unaccountable conduct had thrown the entire family. Remember, I am now writing of events a year old, and if I seem singularly composed, it is only because time has graciously permitted me to grow accustomed to the contemplation of these wonders.

As I listened to the tender whisperings of mother and sister, so full of solicitude and anxiety, an overwhelming sense of my own enforced duplicity took possession of me. Who and what was I that I should have entered ghost-like into this happy family circle, bringing sorrow and suffering to all its members and unwarrantedly usurping the place of the eldest son; turning him from his bride, driving him—(the thought flashes like fire upon my brain) —where is John Sutherland? This is his small, fat white hand I hold before me; this is his heart which I feel beating, but his soul—himself—the man—the being, who called himself Sutherland? Where is he? Was it an exchange of bodies? Between the hours of twelve o'clock last night and seven o'clock that morning I threw off the flesh and form which was my own, and assumed another mortal dwelling place. The occupant of this body— the body which I see staring at me from yonder mirror—abandoned it for mine. It must have been so. And my body— —the external man Jessup—the corporeal shelter which this fond son and loving brother had been forced to enter—what of its fate? Dragged into a prison courtyard and stretched by the neck at the end of a rope, two hours ago.

I do not remember all that occurred in the fever and subsequent delirium which fell upon me. I am told that I lingered between life and death for several months, tenderly watched by the parents and the sister of the unhappy man who died in my place. When I was able to move about, my ignorance of all surroundings, which, as may be imagined, was complete, was attributed by the family physician to a shock of the brain center which, he explained, had destroyed my memory. I must, he said to Mr. and Mrs. Sutherland, be treated as a child and retaught all that I had ever learned. He suggested a trip to Europe, and we are now, after many months, about to sail for England. My failure to recognize the affianced bride of John Sutherland, has, I an told, thrown that young lady into a decline. No member of the Sutherland family has ever crossed the Atlantic, and my intimate knowledge of London will, if I ever reach London, be a new source of wonder to my companions. As for myself, I have passed beyond the reach of wonderment or surprises. I am what I am, while I am, because I am. That is all I know, but I see withal nothing more strange than that any two souls should exchange abiding places than that any individual soul should leave its abiding place tenantless and a prey to worms, as is every day the case in all parts of the world. What guarantee, if I may use so trite an expression, have you, or you, my friend, that the soul, which yields itself nightly to dreamless sleep, will find the same environment upon awakening?

We arrived in New York yesterday from Denver, and as soon as I could decently excuse myself from my "relatives," I went straightway to the Tombs prison on Center Street. Having obtained a card of admission, I entered the inner prison, and made my way to the corridor known as "Murderers' Row." Cell No. 5, my cell, was empty. The jailer, at sight of whom I came near to faint, informed me that Cell No. 5 had not been occupied since one Jessup, the murderer of an Italian, left it for the gallows a year ago.

"And tell me," I inquired with a calmness which amazed me, "how this—this Jessup met this fate?"

"Terrible, terrible, sir," replied the jailer, evidently having, as he spoke, a vivid picture of the scene in his mind. "I never want to see the like of it again. You see, sir, he was a very nervous customer, most extraordinary so, and I expected we'd have trouble with him. But 'long toward midnight he fell into a sleep just like the sleep of a child, and at haif past six he was slumbering as pretty as anything you ever saw. We hated to wake the poor fellow, but it had to be done, so I steps inside the grating and takes hold of his arm. He was awake and bright in a minute. 'All right, Walter,' he says, cheery-like, 'I'm with you.' Then he looks around in a dazed sort of way, and says he, 'Why, hello! What the devil's all this?' and looking at me, he says, 'Who are you? I told him as kindly as I could, that it was time to be going. He was on his feet then, and staring around. 'Well,' says he, 'this may be a very pretty joke the boys have played on me, old man, but I don't like it. I suppose this is the county jail, and I'm in West Denver, hey? The boys must have got me pretty full at Charpiot's, and yet I could almost swear that I went home straight.'

"I saw at once that he was crazy, and I thought it would be a mercy to get through the business as soon as possible; so I called in the deputies, and we read him the death warrant. At times he'd laugh, and then he'd look sort of dazed and wild-like. After the reading, I told him we'd have to be moving, and that I would be obliged to pinion his arms. 'All right, old man,' he said; 'everything goes; but I'll get even with those fellows when their time comes, you mark my words. I suppose now,' he said with a laugh, 'you're going to haul me up?' Tell you, sir," continued the jailer, "it made the cold shivers run down my back to hear him so joking-like, just as if it was all a bit of fun. When we had his arms tied we started for the yard. There was a priest with him, at whom he laughed, saying, 'Well, the boys seem to want to make it as real as possible.' After we got into the court behind the prison, where the gallows stood, and he saw the squad of police and the reporters and deputy sheriffs, he began to tremble, and then suddenly, in a voice that I can hear to this day, he screamed, 'What does it mean? Help! Murder! Murder!' As quick as possible we got him under the drop and pulled the black cap over his face; and then I think he fainted, for he cried 'Julie! Father!' and fell down in a heap. The work was well done, and he didn't suffer much; but I can tell you, sir, I don't want to have to hang any more crazy men."

Well, as I said before, we are off for Europe in the morning, but I do not think I shall ever reach the other side. I have an idea that somewhere about midway of the Atlantic I shall drown this brown bearded man whom everybody calls "John Sutherland."

1-73